TREASURE OF THE
SANGRE DE CRISTOS

TREASURE OF THE

Tales and

With Paintings by JOE BEELER

SANGRE DE CRISTOS

Traditions of the Spanish Southwest

By ARTHUR L. CAMPA

Foreword by J. MANUEL ESPINOSA

UNIVERSITY OF OKLAHOMA PRESS : NORMAN

To my wife, Lucille

By Arthur L. Campa

Spanish Workbook for High School and College
  (Albuquerque, 1934)
Practical Handbook of Spanish Commercial Correspondence
  (joint author with George Sanchez) (New York, 1943)
Mastering Spanish (New York, 1945)
Acquiring Spanish (New York, 1946)
Spanish Folkpoetry in New Mexico (Albuquerque, 1946)
*Treasure of the Sangre de Cristos: Tales and Traditions of the
  Spanish Southwest* (Norman, 1963)
Hispanic Culture in the Southwest
  (Norman, 1979)

Library of Congress Cataloging-in-Publication Data

Campa, Arthur L. (Arthur Leon), 1905–1978.
    Treasure of the Sangre de Cristos : tales and traditions of the
Spanish Southwest / by Arthur L. Campa ; foreword by J.
Manuel Espinosa ; with paintings by Joe Beeler.
        p.   cm.
    Previously published: 1963.
    Includes bibliographical references and index.
    ISBN 0-8061-1176-3
    1. Sangre de Cristo Mountains (Colo. and N.M.)—Social
life and customs.   2. Spaniards—Sangre de Cristo Mountains (Colo. and N.M.)—Folklore.   3. Treasure-trove—Sangre de Cristo Mountains (Colo. and N.M.)   4. Tales—Sangre
de Cristo Mountains (Colo. and N.M.)   I. Title.
F802.S35C36   1994
978.8'49—dc20   94-8093
                                                              CIP

FOREWORD

THIS NEW PAPERBACK EDITION of the late Arthur L. Campa's *Treasure of the Sangre de Cristos: Tales and Traditions of the Spanish Southwest,* first published in 1963, is, in effect, a brand new book for a new generation of readers interested in stories about buried treasure in the Spanish Southwest. Treasure hunting is an activity of perennial popular interest, and readers will enjoy these tales of exciting searches for buried treasure in the mountain areas of New Mexico, a region along the Rio Grande and north of the Mexican border. All the tales have a remarkable freshness because the author, himself an active participant, made on-the-spot investigations and consulted extensively with local old-timers well informed about the many clues relevant to the sites, some in very remote locations.

The history of buried treasure has fascinated readers about the Spanish Southwest since the first Spanish explorers visited the region early in the sixteenth century. The search for gold was a principal motivation for Spanish explorers who scoured the region, without much success, in the sixteenth century, and off and on throughout the Spanish colonial period. When the United States conquered New

Mexico and the surrounding area, Anglo-Americans moved in and introduced important social and cultural changes, but the Spanish-speaking people residing there remembered the many tales handed down from one generation to another as a part of their Spanish cultural heritage. Among these were stories of buried treasure, and many of these local stories became a part of the folklore of the region.

The scope of folklore is of such magnitude that attempts to portray it can be very perplexing. It embraces all branches of popular knowledge that are in a great measure distinct from technical science. Aurelio M. Espinosa defined folklore as "the direct expression of the psychology of mankind from its primitive origins to the present day, transmitted across the ages without the help of technical science. Those traditional elements or factors of civilization that are an important part of the spirit of peoples, that are transmitted from generation to generation, spontaneously, instinctively so to speak . . . are all important in cultural studies. In these elements of human behavior that constitute tradition, the character, the feelings, the manners and customs, the religious beliefs, the artistic powers, and, in short, the ideas of people are documented." (*The Folklore of Spain in the American Southwest,* ed. J. Manuel Espinosa, 2d ed. [Norman: University of Oklahoma Press, 1990], 67.)

The folklore of the Spanish Southwest, like that of other areas, is thus a part of world folklore, and like that of other areas that have undergone cross-cultural experiences over the centuries, it has passed through steps of evolution. Each successive period adds subtle new elements, sometimes mixing the old and the new, including some outside influences but generally evolving under the influence of the local environment. Campa's interesting stories are but one aspect of the broad history of Spanish folk tradition in the American Southwest.

It is fortunate that Campa gathered most of the data for this book in the early decades of this century, for the tales he relates were still fresh in the minds and memories of many old-timers he consulted. Subsequent generations remember little of what Campa's informants possessed. Equally important, many landmarks and geographic features that were Campa's guideposts have been erased by the years.

In some of the stories in which Campa was a major participant, his accounts are so vivid that he leads the reader to believe that he and his enterprising companions had identified all the necessary clues, and they might well have succeeded in accomplishing their goal if only they had been able to make one more final effort with the help of adequate, modern, mechanized earth-moving equipment.

Treasure of the Sangre de Cristos, a classic of its kind, will appeal to folklorists and treasure-hunters. Part of a relatively recent past, the stories in this book have a current freshness about them that adds to their charm.

J. MANUEL ESPINOSA
February 1994

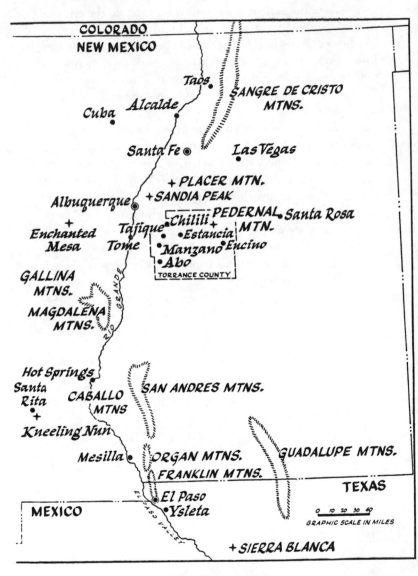

TREASURE LAND

PREFACE

THE TELLER OF A FOLKTALE, unlike the informant who gives
a brief account of events rather than a narrative, reveals part of
his life, part of his accumulated experience as he relates what tradition has willed him together with what he has woven around
this heritage. Eventually, a true storyteller comes to believe what
he has told and retold because he has put part of his own thinking into the narrative to the point where the story becomes his
own property. This is the process that carries traditions from one
generation to another in an unbroken though somewhat tortu-
ous line. This is also the manner in which variants of the same
story are produced.

Whatever the variations and changes made by the storyteller may be, it is fundamentally essential that he know what
he talks about and that he tell it naturally and interestingly. Good
storytellers, like good writers, are not very abundant, but there
are enough of them among the folk to keep tales and legends alive
and rejuvenated. Nothing is more enjoyable than to sit by the
fire in winter, or under the shade of a cottonwood tree in summer, to listen to an ageless *viejo* slowly lead into his narrative
through a series of associations, such as the arrival of the railroad, an Indian attack, a storm, or a hunting trip. These events
always "remind" him of the time when some *compadre* nearly

froze to death in a blizzard, or the time when a she-bear chased the two down a mountain, or the time they found a cave, and so on.

Some of the stories included in this book I heard from the lips of Southwestern storytellers while sitting in the patio of a Texas rancho as a very young boy. After the men were through with the routine chores of feeding the cattle and horses for the night, shutting up the pigs, and seeing that the chickens were safely out of the coyote's reach, the entire family including visitors and hired hands would congregate in the front patio of the house to enjoy a couple of hours of what little coolness there was in the summer air, and talk about anything and everything that came up in the conversation. At this time of the evening one could go to almost any rancho down the Río Grande and find the adults sitting on chairs and the children on the ground, with no more light than the occassional flare of a cigarette from those who smoked.

The only discomfort to these delightful evening gatherings was the hordes of humming mosquitoes hovering around in search of whatever section of skin was exposed. There was no control of these pests at that time; one either became inured to their sting or kept both hands ready to slap them. The counter-attacks were punctuated with all sorts of expletives, depending upon the make-up of the gathering. One way of discouraging these preying night-flyers was a chore usually assigned to the children. A wheelbarrow was piled high with dry manure, lighted, and placed windward where the breeze would carry the pungent smoke into the assemblage and drive away the pesky mosquitoes. I recall that by the time the group broke up and got ready for bed, there was a very noticeable smoky scent about the clothes, but one got used to it and actually came to like the familiar aroma.

In the midst of these surroundings, seated on the ground, I listened to many long accounts about the Santa Fe trade, Indian fights, and treasure hunts, which some ranchero told in the droning deep voice of the outdoor man. Oftentimes, neighbors riding past would drop in right in the middle of a story and ruin what had started out to be an enjoyable evening for the children. I suppose the effect is the same today with an interrupted television program. On the whole, however, and looking back at the "intruders" who broke the thread of a narrative in progress, I now realize that these visitors gave me an opportunity to become acquainted with the *gente* of west Texas in the era of transition from the buckboard to the automobile.

There were run-of-the-mill folks for the most part, people who talked about crops, livestock, and weather, but there were also interesting characters in a natural, matter-of-fact way. I recall an old German by the name of Mauer who lived on the ranch adjoining ours. His presence was always preceded by the smell of an enormous meerschaum, the stem-end in his mouth and the bull's-head-bowl in the hollow of his thick-fingered hand. I was impressed by the gold chain on the bull's nose attached to Señor Mauer's vest but never got close enough to the old man to finger it. When he sat down, his bushy whiskers reached to the end of the long-stemmed pipe, and his thunderous voice made up for his deficiencies in both English and Spanish. His stories were usually humorous, though pointed, commentaries on political and military figures of the day, but his favorite subject was "Chermany." He had never forgotten the fatherland and continued to lead a German existence in Texas with his hard-working, sunbonneted wife and two giant sons, Herman and Willie. When he was talking, no one could interrupt him; his voice would drown out any attempt to take the floor. He never took his wife anywhere, and she made no attempt to learn English or Spanish, but her *kuchen*-filled cupboard was open to any boy or girl who would ask for some in German.

There was also Don Sabino, a little old man with a white beard who always wore *chaparreras* and carried a Winchester in the scabbard of his saddle. He wore a battered and shapeless Stetson and a red *mascada* or kerchief around his neck stained with honest sweat. Whenever the little *vaquero* came to call, he sat on the fringe of the group after the usual *"Buenas Noches"* and remained silent, rolling one cigarette after another until the gathering broke up. Don Sabino lived alone in a one-room abode not far from the Loma Tewa Ranch where he worked, but aside from this single fact no one ever learned much about him. When the evening was over, he would rise, dust the seat of his pants, and ride away at a fast gallop into the night as though he were on his way to something more important than the bunk he slept in.

Don Pancho Fierro was a contrast in every way to the little cowpuncher in woolly chaps. Instead of the broom-tailed sorrel of Don Sabino, Don Pancho rode a gaited bay so sensitive that the least movement of the rider would send it off like a shot. Don Pancho Fierro, the alcalde or ditch-boss as the job was called in Texas, was a man reared in the tradition of the Mexican horseman. He rode tall in the saddle of his *bayo* and could turn on a dime, or ride the narrowest ditch-bank from the main canal to the last rancho on his beat. The alcalde was a gentleman of the saddle, a now-extinct type, a real *caballero,* who knew and observed all the courtesies of a Southwestern horseman. He never rode a horse into the front yard; he stopped by a hitching post or a tree and tied his mount; and when he reached the front door he asked permission of the lady of the house to enter with his spurs on. When he met his friends riding by, he would bring his horse to a stop and lift his hat in greeting to the ladies. Upon leaving the house, he walked his horse a few paces away, waved his hand in a *despedida,* and broke into an easy trot. I always wished he would let me ride his spirited bay but I never asked him because in conversation he had said one day, "There are three things a man should never lend: his wife, his gun, and his horse."

From the old timers whom I met in my childhood, and from those whom I sought out later, when collecting folklore became part of my profession, I have gathered the tales and legends appearing in this book. Fortunately, I had grown up and lived in a bi-cultural atmosphere where the traditions of the Southwest were expressed in both English and Spanish. In this region, one must of necessity be conversant in these two cultures in order to grasp the meanings that do not reveal themselves easily in translation. Additional facts had to be learned from such sources as libraries, newspaper collections, and on-the-scene informants who could supply little-known details. Some stories have been the traditional heritage of my family; here all I had to do was to recall what my mother told me and what I heard from the lips of grandparents, uncles, and aunts. My deepest gratitude goes to them and my sincere thanks to those who were good enough to provide me with other source material.

Miss J. Vivian Hedgdock, librarian of the New Mexico Highlands University, was particularly useful in providing me with the names of persons who knew about the Hermit of Las Vegas, and also put at my disposal all the material about him available in the library. S. Omar Barker, well known New Mexico Poet and writer from Sapello, allowed me to look over his original manuscript on the Hermit and gave me all the information he had on hand. Mrs. Julian Olmstead, one of my former students at the University of New Mexico, now living in Tucson, contributed an anecdote in connection with the story of El Chato. Mrs. Elizabeth Armendariz, granddaughter of Colonel Albert Fountain of Old Mesilla, New Mexico, was particularly useful in locating the grave of the Hermit and in showing me actual possessions of the recluse. Brother James of St. Michael's College in Santa Fe made available a copy of Charles Wolfe's manuscript on the Hermit. Father Libertini and I spent some delightful hours in El Paso swapping tales and comparing notes on those we know in common. Mr. Joe B. Lake, librarian of the newspaper collection at the University of Texas, was good enough to provide me with a rare news story on the Hermit, which could not be found elsewhere. Don Hipólito Baca, grandson of the man who brought the Hermit to Las Vegas, gave me orally a good deal of what is known about him and much that is not too well known. And lastly, Roland Durand allowed me the use of his story on the Jicarita miners. To all these good people who co-operated so efficiently and so willingly, my most hearty *gracias!*

To the John Simon Guggenheim Memorial Foundation of New York, my grateful thanks for the fellowship, which made possible much of the research and all of the writing that went into this book.

ARTHUR L. CAMPA

Denver, Colorado

CONTENTS

TREASURE OF THE
SANGRE DE CRISTOS

CHAPTER 1

The climate of
treasure and legend

◆

THE EXPANSE of mountain, canyon, and plain that is called the Southwest came into Spanish knowledge through a blend of fact, fiction, and fortuitous circumstances. In 1528 Álvar Núñez Cabeza de Vaca[1] with his Negro slave, Estevan, and a few companions—survivors of the ill-fated Florida expedition of Pánfilo Narváez—were shipwrecked on the Texas coast and wandered through the interior for eight years before reaching the Spanish settlements in Sonora and Sinaloa. On their journey they saw for the first time herds of stately bison bending the tall grass with their bellies in a wide, open land where the sun shone brightly and the stars seemed closer in the clear night sky. There was magnetism in the thin, dry air of this "Unknown North," an attraction that was to beckon men of many nationalities for the next four centuries.

As these first Europeans sat around the campfires, they listened to the Indians tell of a land where there were cities paved with gold and houses with turquoise-studded walls. The sixteenth century was a time to believe in legends. There was precedent, fabulous precedent, in the treasures of Montezuma and in the gold of the Peruvian Incas. The Spaniards tried to

[1] Andrés Perez de Ribas, *Triunfos de Nuestra Santa Fe,* I.

3

learn of the location of these new rich lands, and the red men pointed north.

When Núñez and his companions reached the settlements in 1536, he regaled the ears of eager listeners with what he had seen and heard. Noblemen and peasants were aroused by tales of a Gran Quivira[2] and of Seven Cities of Cíbola, where a *new* Mexico[3] would be won through exploration and military conquest. The Viceroy of Mexico, Antonio de Mendoza, became interested in the dazzling prospects. But first someone must be sent to reconnoiter, someone whose judgment could be trusted to check the stories Álvar Núñez had brought back. Fray Marcos de Niza, a seasoned missionary who had accompanied Pizarro in the conquest of Peru, was selected to lead this exploratory expedition. Estevan was chosen as a guide because he had acquired a knowledge of the kind of people and territory to be visited, he was inured to hardship, and he could probably make friends with the Indians along the way. A number of Indians were sent along as porters and interpreters.

In 1539 the party set out on foot in search of Cíbola, the "Cities paved with gold." Estevan went ahead blazing the trail and sending encouraging news of what he saw by means of crosses which the Indians carried back to Niza to tell him that

[2] Cleve Hallenbeck, *Land of the Conquistadores*, 34. Here it is stated that the name *Quivira* was derived from the Spanish, "Quien vivirá, verá." Actually it is an Arabic word taken over into Spanish, with the meaning "great," as in Guadalquivir (Wadi el Kebir, Great River) and Alcazarquivir (El Ksar Kebir, Great Fortress). El Reino de Quivira meant the Great Kingdom.

[3] Most people assume that the name *New Mexico*, from the Spanish *Nuevo México*, was given to this region to distinguish it from the Mexican republic, thereupon referring to the latter as *Old Mexico*. All that the name *Nuevo México* meant was *another* Mexico, for when the adjective *nuevo* is placed before the noun it means *another*, rather than *new*. The Spaniards of colonial days were hoping to find another, a different Mexico with a wealth equal to that of the Mexico that Cortés had conquered. *See*, however, Fernando Ocaranza, *Establecimientos Franciscanos en el Misterioso Reino de Nuevo México*, 7. Here he

4

all was well. The hardy missionary pressed on, treading the path of a legend he now believed in, encouraged by the increasing size of the crosses. One day a runner arrived dragging a cross the size of a man. They were within grasp of their goal. But success presaged for only a short-lived moment. Another Indian runner arrived on the heels of the cross-bearer with sad news and an ominous warning: Estevan had dreamed of things more elusive than gold and died at the hands of the very Indians he had thought to beguile. He had reached the clustered pueblos of the Zuñis, and here he was killed, some say because he was regarded as a spy, others, because of his propensity to seduce Indian women.

With the dream of Cíbola unrealized, Fray Marcos de Niza was forced to turn back empty-handed. He may have come in sight of the Zuñi villages and looked across the broken plain, where the glowing walls of Hawikuh at sunset convinced him that their golden radiance confirmed the legend of the Seven Cities of Cíbola. This unexpected ending to his quest turned back the good friar with an even greater dream, one that he passed on to those who were to follow his trail.[4] And many followed, including such great explorers as Don Francisco Vásquez de Coronado, who led in 1540–41 the most colorful expedition ever seen in the Southwest;[5] Juan de Oñate; and others, who

gives a quotation without author which reads: "Antonio de Espejo en al año de 1528 descubió 15 Provincias todas llenas de gran número de Indios y pueblos con casas de 4 y 5 altos. A quien pusieron por nombre el Nuevo México, por parecerse en muchas cosas al viejo."

[4] Fray Marcos de Niza has elicited eulogies as well as adverse criticism from different historians. Some refer to him as a hardy, courageous padre and others call him the biggest liar that ever lived. Whatever the case may be, the fact remains that he was an adventurous pioneer who trod on foot more than a thousand miles through virgin territory without the aid of maps.

[5] There were two hundred armored knights, seventy crossbowmen, eight hundred Indians, and a long pack train loaded with baggage and supplies.

5

tried to locate the treasures Álvar Núñez had talked about in 1536.

Even today the adventure of the treasure-trail is not over. Despite the lapse of centuries, the embers of tradition glow hot again when men speak of lost mines or hidden treasure in the old Southwest. The myth of the Seven Cities died early in Spanish colonial times when it was discovered that they were nothing but the mud and stone huts of Pueblo Indians. But imagined sites of ancient Quivira in New Mexico are honeycombed with diggings where men to the present day search for the fabled wealth that lured Coronado in 1540.

The scene has shifted to some villages east of Albuquerque named Chilili, Tajique, and Manzano, where even people claiming to be descendants of Walt Whitman spent years exploring a cave where the treasure of Quivira is supposed to be hidden. There is also a story about a Gypsy driving six white horses, who paid the residents of Tajique to dig for the treasure from a map in his possession. When it was located and about to be uncovered, he plied all the men with quantities of wine in celebration of their great fortune, and in the dark of night he stole away never to be heard from again, and the treasure went with him. The three ruined cities of Abo, Quarai, and Tabira are also sites of this fabulous treasure "infinitely better known, in this day of grace and putative light, than the 'Gran Quivira,' " said Charles F. Lummis in 1893.[6] In New Mexican territorial days there was a ten-thousand-dollar reward for the finding of Quivira, but no one ever collected.

To the original legend has been added traditions of lost Spanish mines. Old prospectors sit around looking at maps and study-

[6] "The Cities That Were Forgotten," *Scribner's Magazine*, Vol. 13, No. 4 (April 1893). Here Lummis reviewed the history of the many conquerors and travelers who had given ear to the treasure story of Quivira from Coronado in 1540 to Dominguez de Mendoza in 1684.

ing the terrain hoping to find a clue that will lead them to the opening of a cave or to some shaft covered with brush and now overgrown with trees. Others devise electronic instruments to lead them directly to the site of hidden gold. Every mountain range from the Guadalupes in western Texas to the Sierras of California, from the barren hills of Chihuahua to the timbered Rockies of Colorado harbors countless tales of untold treasures, outlaws' caches, and lost mines of which the stacked bullion would provide many a king's ransom.

The ingredients from which legends are forged in oral tradition abound in the Southwest. There is a curious blend of realism, fantasy, and intrigue. Tradition colors and embellishes these accounts with the romance of moonlit nights and feminine wiles, but for the most part the stories deal with the struggle of men against nature, men against men trying to find the way to the end of the rainbow. The ingredients which tradition has forged into a maze of legends have come from the romance of the Spanish conqueror, from the Indian on the warpath, from the mule trains over the *Camino Real*,[7] from the Santa Fe Trail, from the fabulous strikes of the Real de Santa Eulalia in northern Chihuahua, and from the eighty-thousand-dollar nugget in New Mexico's "Bridal Chamber."[8] These are the raw materials of tradition, to which we must add the circumstance of war.

Men from all walks of life and from many nations have become part of the Southwest. There have been explorers, trappers,

[7] *El Camino Real* was the name used to designate the highway or trail from Santa Fe to Chihuahua; but this name ("Royal Highway") became synonymous with *main highway* in Spanish, and even at the beginning of the paved highway era surfaced roads in the American Southwest were referred to by stockmen and farmers as "El Camino Real," to distinguish them from unpaved country roads.

[8] The lake valley region south of Hillsboro, New Mexico, was one of the best ore producers in the Southwest, according to Joseph Miller, *New Mexico: A Guide to the Colorful State*. The romance connected with mining is

7

prospectors, soldiers of fortune, and finally peaceful settlers in search of new homes. There have also been men and women whose unlawful activities left behind uncharted treasure, the whereabouts of which is grist for the mill of tradition. Many tons of earth have been moved searching for the treasures of Father La Rue, El Chato, the Jesuits of Bamoa, and lately Pancho Villa, to mention only a few of the best known.

There is fiction and there is fantasy in the legendary traditions of the Southwest, but there is also enough credible fact found, enough evidence uncovered from time to time to keep the interest alive and roll the story along on people's tongues. Men have tried to unravel fact from fiction in their attempts to locate a hidden trove. Occasionally some have come across an abandoned mine or a cave while in search of something else. Demetrio Varela of El Paso was one of these men favored by fortune who enjoyed the thrill of running his hands over stacks of gold bullion.

---

illustrated by the story of two miners who in the early eighties struck an ore vein and promptly sold out for one hundred thousand dollars. Two days later the vein ran into what is known as the "Bridal Chamber," a subterranean cavity that produced over three million dollars in horn silver.

8

CHAPTER 2

Lost Mines in
The Organ Mountains

◆

THERE ARE PEOPLE living in El Paso today who still wonder at the experience of Don Demetrio, as they refer to the old prospector who died peacefully at home there during World War I. Demetrio Varela was born in southern New Mexico when that section of the country was still part of Mexico and lived under the Mexican, Confederate, and American flags. He left the family farm in the Mesilla Valley and went to work in the mines of Sierra Blanca east of El Paso when he was still a young boy, but had to return home at the outbreak of the Civil War. As young Demetrio was not particularly fond of farming, at least not enough to work the small acreage the family owned, he began to look around for something else to do until he hit upon cattle-tracking, a skill he learned from one of the survivors of the Senecú Indians.[1] Instead of tracking down lodes of ore, he began

---

[1] The cattle industry throughout Latin America developed many features and occupations that were pretty uniform throughout the length of the continent. One of these was the *rastreador,* the tracker of whom Sarmiento speaks as a type of Argentinian gaucho. In the Southwest this personage was quite prominent, particularly in New Mexico where the local Indians were used as *rastreadores* or *huelleros* because they were better acquainted with the country. They were on call like a doctor or a midwife, and their arrival at a ranch where stock had been stolen or had run away was as important as that of any professional man. One of the last of these trackers was an old Senecú Indian, who

tracking down stolen cattle in the days when rustling was the full-time occupation of cattle thieves. He would have preferred mining or prospecting, but there was little of that around the sleepy valley; however, his newly found trade was a good substitute and he worked at it so well that in a short time he earned a reputation as the best *rastreador* or *huellero* from Mesilla to the Mexican border.

Demetrio's skill with cattle and horses eventually led him to a permanent job as *mayordomo* of a ranch belonging to a young widow by the name of Doña Chonita, whose late husband had left her some very good livestock and a considerable parcel of land. Things went along smoothly for a few years until an extended drought ruined the crops of the rancho and thinned out the stock. Many of the farmers who depended on the Río Grande for irrigation were wiped out, and even Doña Chonita, who was better off than most, had to let her ranch hands go one at a time. Only Demetrio, the *mayordomo,* remained to look after her diminished property hoping to make a comeback when times got better. Despite his added responsibilities he did not overlook his own interests, for by the end of the year he married his employer. Hard times continued to plague him and his wife to the point where he was compelled to go back to mining and cattle-tracking.

Late in the winter of 1878, a well-known *hacendado* by the name of Armijo had some of his prize cattle stolen by rustlers in Old Mesilla. The wealthy rancher remembered the reputation of Demetrio and sent for him to retrieve the stolen stock. This was easier said than done, but the fee which the old Don offered was attractive to the *rastreador* even though the thieves already

---

lived in Ysleta, Texas, south of El Paso. As late as 1918 the old *rastreador* was called in on a case involving the rustling of a prize Holstein bull that had been taken from the ranch of Doña Martina in San Jose. He followed the trail for three days and recovered the animal below Fabens by the Mexican border.

had a full day's start. Early in the morning Demetrio set out with two *vaqueros* from the Armijo ranch and picked up the trail by the time the sun was halfway up. At noon the searching party rode into a deep arroyo where the cattle had been butchered and the beef apparently loaded on several pack horses. The trail turned northeast toward the Organ Mountains heading directly for Saint Augustine Pass. Demetrio and his men soon discerned the thieves' plan: they were going to contact another gang over the mountain pass or trade the beef to the Indians for pelts. If the weather held out, the *vaqueros* believed they could overtake the thieves by riding all night, possibly coming upon them as they broke camp at daylight the following day.

The plan would have worked out if the wind, followed by a driving snow, had not come up during the afternoon just as they were reaching Saint Augustine Pass. For awhile all three horsemen pulled down their hats and bent their heads into the blizzard hoping to ride for shelter on the other side of the mountain, but eventually they had to give up their plan and head into the nearest canyon in the Organ Range. No longer hampered by searching for the fast disappearing trail, they spurred their horses toward a clump of pine trees bunched together at the foot of an overhanging ledge where the driving snow could not reach them. By the time they reached the trees the storm had become a blinding blizzard. After tying their horses to the trees the three saddle-tired men entered a well sheltered cove under the rocky ledge where they planned to wait for the storm to spend itself.

In a short while there was a fire going with a pot of steaming coffee, which made them forget how long they had ridden. After a warm meal and several cups of coffee, Demetrio stood up and began to take inventory of the mountain ledge while his two *vaqueros* searched around for dry wood to keep the fire going. Demetrio's prospecting savvy soon found what looked

like an opening covered with rocks and debris a few feet from camp. He pushed aside several big rocks and tree branches until he uncovered an opening large enough to allow him to slip into what appeared to be a natural cave. As he disappeared into the dark recess, the *vaqueros* sitting around the campfire shouted: "Look out, Demetrio! Careful you don't run into a bear!"

He shouted back something which his men did not hear as he crawled into the opening. He worked his way in, and soon reached a place where he could stand without bumping his head on the roof of the cave. He pulled out of his pocket a candle *cabito*. He always carried this home-made tallow candle along with his flint whenever he went out; it was part of a prospector's equipment, which came in handy in cases like this. His candle lighted, Demetrio, now turned prospector, was ready to make a closer inspection of the interior. To his surprise it was not a natural cave as he had thought at first; there were timber supports still standing along the walls and the telltale marks of the miner's pick were evident. He made slow progress examining the walls, being careful not to cause a slide of crumbling rocks, or fall into an open shaft. For about twenty paces the tunnel went straight into the mountain; then it turned sharply to the left and sloped downward noticeably. At this point the flame of the candle began to sputter and blow toward him indicating a current of air coming from some opening at the other end of the cave. Holding the candle as high as the roof would allow, he continued to explore, more carefully now because the air felt moist and the floor was wet and slippery in places.

Demetrio was trying to figure out who might have worked this mine, for it was definitely a mine, when he caught sight of something that made him come to a sudden stop and reach for his gun. A figure about four feet high was huddled close to the side of the cave. He watched closely, ready to fire at the first move, but the vaguely outlined figure stood still. He remembered the warning given him in jest by the *vaqueros* as he entered the cave; a bear was something he would rather not meet in these close quarters, although he had met bears before and was acquainted with their fighting habits. With his gun in one hand and the candle held high with the other, he approached the dark object cautiously one step at a time. Nothing seemed to move against the wall. Gradually as he approached, the thing took form and no longer seemed dangerous; it was only a stack of rawhide sacks covered with a heavy accumulation of fine dust.

Demetrio put the gun back into the holster, brushed away the dust from the stack, and with his hunting knife cut loose the thong tied around the mouth of the top sack. The contents, held back for untold years, cascaded to the ground at the feet of a very surprised and excited explorer. He picked up one of the larger pieces of ore and held the candle close where he could examine it. There were unmistakable veins of yellow running through the quartz. *"Caramba!"* was the only thing Demetrio could say, but he repeated it again and louder when he came upon a second stack a few paces farther on in the cave. It was a smaller stack or appeared so because it was partly sunk into the ground. He picked up a heavy small bar from the top, shook it, and blew off the dust. With his hunting knife he scraped the surface and revealed the yellow metal he had prospected for all his life.

Now, deep in a cave which he hadn't known existed and for which he hadn't been looking, he found a stack of gold bars lying before him. He was stunned by the sudden prospect of wealth, too overcome to do much except poke with his hunting knife around the stack wondering how long the gold bars had lain underground.

A few paces beyond the stack the prospector came to a wide clearing in the cave where a forge and an ore-crusher had been installed. Like a boy who has found a new toy, he pulled on the bellows arm, and the stiff leather cracked under the pressure. It was quiet as the traditional grave inside the cave, but Demetrio's ears were ringing with excitement. His first impulse had been to run back to tell his companions outside about the fortune he had just found, but by the time he looked over the underground layout he changed his mind and went back to sit by the stack of bullion.

Demetrio rolled a cigarette and sat back on his boot heels

to smoke, musing over his treasure, thinking of the people who had worked so hard to produce it. He stood up when the cigarette burned his fingers. He ran his hands several times over the bars like a little boy running a stick along a picket fence. Finally he picked up two bars, wiped off the dust on his pants leg, stuck them carefully under his shirt, and made them fast with his belt, before returning to join his men under the rock ledge. The discovery he had made in the cave had caused him completely to lose track of time. When he came out into the open, he was surprised to see all but an improvised shelter of pine boughs covered with a heavy blanket of snow. The *vaqueros* had gathered a good supply of wood for the night, and the campfire burned cozily, protected by the clump of pine trees and shielded by the projecting rock ledge. As Demetrio approached the campfire almost blinded by the light after his long stay in the dark interior of the cave, the two men shouted at him:

"Hombre! We were getting ready to go in and drag you out. What happened? Were you caught in a land slide?"

Demetrio simply told them that the going was slow inside the cave and that it had taken him more time than he had realized exploring and looking around at rock formations. The three men sat around the fire *platicando,* spinning yarns and making interesting conversation the way Spanish peasants have been doing for centuries.

The following morning they decided to return to the ranch; the thieves had put a blizzard and two days between them, disposed of the beef, and were out of reach. As they made their way back to Mesilla, Demetrio had little to say; he was lost in thought planning for a way to return to his treasure when the weather would improve in early spring. By the time he returned home his mind was made up.

Doña Chonita noticed how pensive Demetrio had become

since his return from the tracking expedition but attributed his mood to the failure to find the thieves and the cattle.

"Don't worry, *viejo*," she consoled him. "After all, Don Armijo can't expect you to perform miracles. Besides, there was the storm that kept you from going any farther."

Demetrio wanted to tell his wife what he had found but he decided to wait and surprise her when he brought the first load of gold bars. Besides, she might unwittingly let out the secret and have every man in the valley looking for the treasure.

It was difficult for a man with such a secret to sit around the house and not be able to do anything about it. It was therefore a relief when his *compadres* came around a few days after his return to remind him of a mining claim they had staked out in Sierra Blanca early in the fall. He went along with the party to be gone about two months at most. This would give him plenty of time to work out a plan whereby he could go back to the cave on some pretext and haul out the stack of bars before anyone else could discover what he was up to.

About two weeks after arriving at the claim in Sierra Blanca, Don Demetrio suffered the gravest accident in his life. A shot he was lighting went off prematurely and the explosion drove flecks of sharp shale into both his eyes blinding him completely. He was taken to a hospital in El Paso, but despite all efforts he failed to regain his sight. The long convalescence drove all thoughts of the cave from his mind, but when he was taken back to Mesilla, he told his wife about it for the first time. She listened, as she had always listened to his enthusiastic stories about claims where they would strike it rich some day: just another tale of the many that old prospectors like to tell their listeners. Eventually, Doña Chonita died and Don Demetrio was taken by his kin to live in El Paso, where he sat under a spreading mulberry tree in the patio of the house and told over and over again the wonderful story of the mine in Los Órganos. Leaning on his cane as he sat, the white-haired nonagenarian never tired of relating how one day he stood before a stack of solid gold bullion in a cave in the Organ Mountains.

Shortly before his death, Don Demetrio earned a small but satisfying reward for the knowledge he had of the lost mine. A party of eastern treasure-hunters came to the old prospector with a very interesting request. He was to accompany them and retrace the trail he had taken in 1878 when trailing the stolen cattle of the Armijo ranch. The old man agreed. On the appointed day they started from the original site of the ranch, and following his description of the terrain they rode northeast from Mesilla to the foot of the Organ Mountains. For two days they searched over the mountainside for the overhanging ledge and the clump of pine trees, but nothing resembling the landmark was ever found. The trees had long disappeared and the place where the ledge was supposed to be was washed smooth by water and wind erosion. It was the end of the trail for the eastern fortune seekers and also the end of a disappointing trail for a ninety-seven-year-old prospector-*rastreador*.

Had Don Demetrio stumbled upon the lost Padre mine of Father La Rue, or part of El Chato's loot? One can only conjecture, for all these treasures are said to be buried somewhere between Mount Franklin in El Paso and the Caballo and San Andres ranges in southern New Mexico.

We do know from what little history is available that Father La Rue, La Cruz, or Le Ruz, as tradition variously calls him, came to the New World from Europe, the son of a well-to-do farmer in southern France. According to some sources, he was originally named Philip. Some say that in the French tradition one must also *cherchez la femme* in the life of La Rue, for in his youth he was very much in love with a girl named Marie, of

whom his father disapproved because she could not bring suffi-
cient dowry. Disappointed over this unhappy circumstance,
young Philip entered the army for a few years, at the end of
which he returned to find Marie married. In order to sever all
connections with his unhappy past, he changed his name to La
Rue and entered a monastery. At the conclusion of his studies he
was sent to Mexico and eventually was assigned to a small settlement north of Durango.

For a number of years La Rue ministered to a hardship-
ridden outpost where soldiers serving in the northern provinces
of Mexico stopped on the way back to Mexico City. One of these
was an old campaigner too spent and tired to continue the trip
southward. During his short stay in the village, he became a
close friend of the kind young priest and before dying gave him
the secret location of a very rich lode, which he had just found
during his military service in the north. After the death of the
old soldier, La Rue proposed to his small band of followers a
move to the location of the mine supposedly hidden in southern
New Mexico. The group did not hesitate to leave their miserable
outpost; and without consulting his superiors in Durango, La
Rue helped them load their scant belongings and started for
New Mexico. They journeyed "four days beyond El Paso del
Norte to a mountain range called Los Órganos," as the directions given by the soldier read, and located the mine near Saint
Augustine Pass in Soledad Canyon between Espiritu Santo
Springs and La Cueva de las Vegas overlooking the Mesilla Valley. In a few weeks the colony began to work the rich vein they
had located, extracting and refining ore, at first with a crudely
made *arrastra,* later with a forge and bellows fashioned from
buffalo hides. No one in the sparsely populated region knew of
the existence of the colony, much less of their mining activities,
except an occasional Indian who was quickly dispatched by the

guards at the village when he ventured too near their hideout.

Every month or so a couple of men with a pack train were sent to Mesilla to procure supplies paid for with gold from the mine. In those days of limited currency no one asked questions so long as gold was offered in any form, and the traders did not volunteer any information. Meanwhile the authorities in Durango decided to inquire about La Rue's colony in northern Mexico through a man called Maximiliano. He found the place abandoned and when he inquired further north in Parral he was told that a small group of travelers in the company of a priest had passed by many years before. In El Paso del Norte too Maximiliano was given the same information, and so he proceeded northward to the village of Mesilla. By this time he suspected that the Apaches had been responsible for the disappearance of Father La Rue. No one had ever heard the name or seen the band, which supposedly had left El Paso some years previously.

He was about to return south when a pack train arrived in Mesilla to pick up supplies, as was customary with La Rue's colony. Thinking that these men might know something about the priest, Maximiliano inquired from the two in charge of the mule train, but they shook their heads and said they had never heard of anyone by that name. The merchant in the village store told Maximiliano that these men came about once a month to buy supplies, but he never knew where they came from and when asked they gave evasive answers. Maximiliano was interested to learn that these same men paid for their supplies with gold dust, and that they usually bought enough supplies to keep a good-sized group of people.

When the men returned to the hideout in the Organ Mountains, they reported to La Rue the presence of a stranger who had questioned them very insistently in Mesilla about La Rue and his colony. Early the following morning, Maximiliano, who had trailed the pack train the night before, appeared in person at the hidden village requesting that the production of the mine be turned over to him in the name of the Church. La Rue explained that the people in the village were the sole owners of what they mined and that he could not dispose of property that did not belong to him. Maximiliano insisted that as their leader the priest was obligated to turn over the gold to the Church, but Father La Rue stood firm and refused to give up a single nugget.

The colony heard no more about Maximiliano until early one morning, when they saw a column of soldiers approaching the mountain hideout. As soon as the lookout guards gave the alarm, the villagers carried all their gold to a secret hiding place, covered the mine completely, and waited for the soldiers to arrive. The commander of the troops laid siege to the village and ordered La Rue to turn over the gold, but the soldiers never found the gold they had come to take nor the source from whence it came. The mine had been thoroughly concealed and the battle that followed La Rue's refusal to surrender the gold never revealed the hiding place.

There are men living today who claim to be descendants of La Rue's colony. They escaped because they were children at the time of the battle, but although they speak knowingly about their ancestors' wealth they have no idea of its location. From time to time the Organ Mountains yield small pieces of quartz with rich traces of gold as an ironic reminder that the precious metal is still there. Some of these specimens were found by Colonel George A. Baylor during the Civil War, but a diligent search with the help of his soldiers failed to disclose the source. Colonel Albert J. Fountain of Mesilla is supposed to have found some documents in the Doña Ana Mission telling of a rich mine covered up by a sudden cloudburst, and George Griggs writing about Mesilla many years later suggests that a lump of black quartz heavy with gold which the Colonel had in his possession may have played an important part in his mysterious disappearance on his last ride over the Organ Mountains.[2]

Father La Rue has not been allowed to rest quietly in his grave, and until his fabulous hoard is found people will continue to talk about him and his mine. One of the latest attempts to locate the treasure is described by Henry James in his book, *The Curse of San Andres*. This author tells of a doctor named Noss who on November 7, 1937, discovered a deep fissure in Soledad Peak at the southern end of the San Andres Mountains in Hembrillo Basin. According to his story, the doctor brought up from a chasm in the rock eighty-six gold bars with a value of from three thousand to six thousand dollars apiece. There were also some interesting manuscripts signed by the pope, in addition to some trinkets and the usual mining paraphernalia. In trying to make the deep cache more accessible, the doctor set off a charge of dynamite and this caused a cave-in that buried the only known access to the treasure.

Dr. Noss was murdered in 1949, and the same year his stepson, Marvin Beckwith, crashed with his airplane and died while attempting to make a landing on the Hembrillo Basin near the location.

On April 3, 1953, the following item appeared in one of the Albuquerque papers:

The state has given Mrs. Ova M. Noss three months more to hunt

[2] Colonel Albert J. Fountain, a former army officer married to one of the leading Spanish families in Old Mesilla, New Mexico, was on his way from a court session in Lincoln where he had been prosecuting cases against cattle thieves of the Rustlers War in the late seventies. He was driving a wagon with his twelve-year-old son and was last seen at Apache Wells. From the tracks discovered by the posse sent out of Las Cruces, his wagon had been driven off the road with the horses at full gallop. Only the wrecked wagon and his ripped traveling bags were found. The disappearance of Colonel Fountain and his young boy is one of New Mexico's unsolved mysteries.

for a fabulous treasure she believes is hidden in a huge cave in south-central New Mexico . . . worth as much as 22 million.

But operations at the site are complicated today by the fact that it is located within the White Sands Proving Grounds, and the federal government refuses to grant permission to enter.

In the spring of 1953 a story appeared in the Denver papers telling of my interest in treasure tales. A few days later I received an interesting letter from a retired government employee by the name of Frank O. Starr, who wrote from Albuquerque saying: "My hobby and business is Spanish and pre-Spanish treasures and lost mines." Since this was the sort of man I wanted to talk to, the next time I was in Albuquerque I dropped in to see Mr. Starr at his hotel. On one of the many maps covering the walls of his room, he showed me numerous locations of mines and treasures he knew about. He was in partnership with a person who had invented a device for locating precious metals and mineral deposits of all sorts. After a brief description of the machine, he showed me a long list of discoveries corroborating the claims made by "the doctor scientist and his instrument." Among other stories he mentioned the one of "Doc Noss" and Soledad Peak in the San Andres Mountains, adding that he was then negotiating with the late doctor's widow to use his detector to pin-point the exact location of the gold bars at the bottom of the buried cave.

About this same time I received another letter from a man in Loveland, Colorado, named Frank M. Johnson. He too had an instrument which he had assembled and which operated along radio-magnetic principles. In a letter written in the spring of 1953 he stated:

> I know of gold bars in a crack in a small mountain 56 miles southeast of Hot Springs, now called Truth or Consequences. The entrance was sealed and there are eight stacks of bars of gold

in there—1 mummie, a pile of skeleton bones, 2 ox cart wheels. This is now inside the White Sands proving grounds 5 miles.

I received this letter a few months before Henry James' book on the same subject came off the press.

CHAPTER 3

TREASURE-HUNTERS
AND PROSPECTORS

◆

THE SEARCH FOR PRECIOUS METALS in the mountain ranges of the Southwest was officially recognized at an early date. On March 26, 1685, a soldier by the name of Pedro de Abalos filed claim before Don Domingo Jironza Petriz de Cruzate, governor and captain general of New Mexico, for a mine in the "Sierrilla de Fray Cristobal" north of the San Andres Mountains, to which he gave the resounding name of: *Nuestra Señora del Pilar de Saragossa.*[1] In 1709 Juan de Uribarri appeared before Don Joseph Chacon Medina Salazar y Villaseñor, Marqués de las Peñuelas, and governor of New Mexico at that time, to declare a mining location in the northern part of the province.

Josiah Gregg claims that the Indians stipulated in 1692 when Don Diego de Vargas reconquered the province of New Mexico after the revolt of 1680, that the Spaniards were not to engage in

---

[1] This grant is supposed to have been made to a soldier retreating to El Paso after the Pueblo Revolt. *See* Rossiter W. Raymond, *Statistics of Mines and Mining in the Territories West of the Rocky Mountains,* 397.

Although many documents were lost in the Indian revolt of 1680, records subsequent to this date indicate that there had been mining during the early days of New Mexico. Stuart A. Northop, *Minerals of New Mexico,* 9, states that "gold was mined at La Mina de la Tierra in the Cerrillos district . . . and several mines near Picuris Pueblo were registered before Governor Don Joachin Codallos y Robal."

mining. It is also said that the Indians, knowing that mineral wealth was one of the sources of trouble with the Spaniards, covered all the mines they had been working previous to the revolt. The fact that a mine known as *Nuestra Señora de los Reyes de Linares* was reopened in 1713 in the Sierra de San Lazaro, or what is now known as Old Placer Mountains, would definitely indicate that some mines were covered up by the New Mexico Indians.

There is a story in Taos about a Mexican by the name of Vigil who found a document in a church in Guadalajara, Mexico, stating that in 1680 the Spaniards covered up fourteen million pesos' worth of gold in a shaft in the mountains near the pueblo of Taos. This treasure has been hunted by many who believe that the Indians know much more than they are willing to tell. Some of the early prospectors who came to Taos have explored all the likely spots in the area as far as the Red River and into the Moreno Valley, but aside from small locations like the one of a Swede named Gus Lawson, nothing like a Spanish gold hoard has been discovered. In 1953 an Indian from Picuris named Roland Durand, then working at the Ute Agency in Colorado, told in a newspaper interview appearing in *El Crepusculo* of Taos, about two prospectors who started a gold rush to the Jicarita Peak in the Taos Mountains.

According to this story, on July 25, 1863, two Picuris[2] Indians named Juan Gallule and Techato Martínez packed their donkeys and started out on a deer-hunting expedition into the thickly wooded Jicarita. After setting up their camp south of the Peak

[2] Picuris, better known as San Lorenzo Pueblo, is located twenty miles south of Taos, New Mexico. It should not be confused with the village of San Lorenzo near Silver City in the southwestern part of the state. The name Picuris is from the Keresan word *Pikuria* meaning "those who paint." Today the Picuris are mixed with white and Apache; less than a score are said to be of pure Pueblo blood.

25

the Indians separated, not expecting to see anyone in that part of the country. Early in the morning, Gallule smelled smoke and followed the scent until he came upon two burros tethered a short distance from a tent, where a young white man was sitting on a log peeling potatoes. As Gallule approached boldly into camp, the white man gave him a long, hard look and finally said: "Hello, Chief." Gallule who spoke no English, simply answered: *"Way-no, way-no,"* and sat down upon another log facing the tent opening. A second man came from behind the tent with some firewood and proceeded to build a campfire. The thing that caught the attention of the Indian was a heavy pan just inside the entrance of the tent with some white, shiny substance floating on top. One of the men accidentally touched the pan, and then it was that Gallule saw some yellow particles that he took to be gold. He looked at the pan so intently that one of the men got up, casually walked over by the tent, and moved the pan inside where the Indian hunter could no longer see it.

As soon as breakfast was ready, the men invited the Indian to join them; and after the meal was over the older of the two, who appeared to be the father of the younger one, went inside the tent and reappeared with a slab of bacon, which he gave to Gallule. The Indian nodded his thanks, as is customary among the Picuris, and left camp still thinking about the pan and the yellow particles. Instead of going back to his own camp, he backtracked and watched the strangers for the rest of the day. That evening he told his hunting mate, Techato, what he had seen, and after talking it over they both decided to watch the white men. For three days from daybreak until dark, they watched the campers, hoping to trail them to the mine they suspected they were working, but the men simply sat around camp, cooked their meals in the open, and slept like men on vacation.

Gallule was so put out that he was all for shooting them. Said he: "These white men are nothing but suspicious coyotes!" Techato quieted him down by reminding him that in order to find out where they had their mine they needed the men alive. On the fourth day Gallule waited until noon and then decided to drop in on the miners' camp once more to see if he could find some clue to their activities. They greeted him in a more friendly manner this time and invited him to dinner. Before he left he was given another side of bacon, some potatoes, and a plug of chewing tobacco. Again the Indian nodded his thanks, said *"Way-no"* and added *"Adiós"* because he did not intend to return.

The men showed no intention of leaving camp, and so after

27

a few more days' watching, the Indians decided to move their camp farther down where the game was plentiful. Early in the fall the miners broke camp and came down by way of Mora into Las Vegas. From there they continued to Denver and registered at a hotel in the early winter. They never went back to Jicarita, because one morning not long after they came to the hotel, father and son were found dead amidst an assortment of empty whiskey bottles in a room where signs of struggle were still evident. The investigation, according to Durand, disclosed that the men had been drinking heavily and apparently got into an argument, which they settled in frontier fashion.

In going over their personal effects, the authorities found some gold nuggets and a map sewed inside the lining of the father's coat with the name "Jicarita" plainly written on it. On the back of the map there was a legend which read:

> The tools are hidden five hundred feet southwest of the camp on top of a large bushy pine tree. Six hundred feet east of this tree is the opening to the mine covered with poles and dirt topped with moss and grass. The hole is drilled horizontally about ten to fifteen feet wide.

The name "Jicarita" did not mean much to the Denver settlers at that time, but gold nuggets and a map were a familiar language to people who had come west in search of riches. For awhile no one knew whether the place mentioned on the miner's map was in the United States or in Mexico, but when it was learned that Jicarita was a peak near the Indian village of Picuris in northern New Mexico, miners, prospectors, and even geologists, according to the Durand family, swarmed into the village anxious to know where the peak was located. Some of the treasure-seekers offered a good reward to anyone who could guide them to it. Gallule and Techato, the two who had been with the campers on the peak, took several parties to Jicarita around the back side where the camp they were looking for could not be located. Julian Durand, the father of Roland, was then a boy of ten and went along to tend the pack burros they used on the trail. The wild-goose chase ended when the weather closed in, and once again the village returned to its normal peaceful existence.

With the hordes of treasure-seekers gone, the persistent Gallule waited until spring; then he set out, taking young Julian along, but instead of the circuitous trail he had used when he acted as a guide he went directly to the place where he had met the campers. The cinders and ashes of the campfire were still visible, and even the tent stakes they had left behind protruded through a heavy carpet of pine needles. For four days the two Indians searched every tree and every nook and cranny, but they found no trace of the tools nor the mine.

"That coyote's map is a fake!" was Gallule's disgusted exclamation, as they returned to Picuris.

Julian was too young then to be so easily discouraged by their failure, and although he did not go back to the peak for almost fifty years, he always talked about the hidden mine, which some day he would look for. That day did not come until his grown son, Roland, insisted that they form a partnership with someone of means whom they could trust and make a thorough search of Jicarita. In 1923 father and son called on Porfirio Abreu of Peñasco, a Spanish village not far from Picuris, and confided their plan to him. Don Porfirio agreed to their proposition on condition that his brother and uncle be included in the deal.

When the date for the trip was set, Roland went to see his employer, a ranchman by the name of Abraham Smith, in order to get some time off, but since it was a confidential affair he told Smith that he wanted to go fishing. The rancher was short-handed and would not hear of letting Roland go; thus in the end he never made the trip he had engineered and looked forward to for such a long time.

Julian Durand and the Abreus camped for two weeks on Jicarita Peak and inspected every foot of ground and every tree for miles around the miners' camp, but they too returned home empty-handed. Roland Durand in 1953 concluded his account by saying:

> Juan Gallule and Techato Martínez who knew the miners' camp are gone. My dad, Julian A. Durand, who also knew the place and had a great desire to show it to me died before he could do it. The mine is possibly there, but it may be regarded by some as a legend, perhaps as the lost mine of Jicarita.

More factual and less fictional are the discoveries made at Santa Rita in southwestern New Mexico at the beginning of the nineteenth century, although the manner in which these mines were discovered is no less legendary than the stories of those that have been reputedly lost. One account states that in 1800 Colonel José Carrasco, an officer of the Spanish army in Mexico befriended an Indian by some act of kindness, whereupon the grateful Indian volunteered to show him the location of a copper mine, which eventually developed into what is now the mining community of Santa Rita. The Indians of the Southwest had for many years extracted sheets of copper protruding through the granodiorite matrix at that place.

Down in the Organ Mountains, not far from the Mexican border, enough gold and silver has been found to give some credibility to the legend of Father La Rue's rich lode. The silver mines of Organ,[3] discovered in 1849, yielded over one half mil-

---

[3] Both Northrop, *op. cit.*, and Muriel Sibell Wolfe, *The Bonanza Trail: Ghost Towns and Mining Camps of the West,* mention the discoveries of gold in the southern part of New Mexico at Organ and other points of the Caballo Mountains. While it is generally stated that the Indians did not work any mines, there is considerable evidence given by some of the expeditions sent out by

lion dollars' worth of ore by 1904, and the Torpedo Mine discovered later in the mountains produced over one million dollars in the same length of time. The continuation of this same range north to the Caballo Mountains on Highway 85 leads to the Shandon Placers discovered by Encarnación Silva in 1901. No inconsiderable amounts of gold were panned there at the beginning of the present century. And so it goes, fact and fiction alternating and filling in the lapses of time in order to keep up man's insatiable desire to get rich quick.

The Spanish Southwest is a land where for many years fact and fiction have blended inexorably into a reality that does not easily draw the line between these two factors. It may be because it is a land where imaginary events, like the "Kneeling Nun of San Vicente," become accepted as actualities, where facts are molded rather than altered by the mellowing force of oral tradition. In this sparsely populated region of the United States, solitude invites daydreaming and the imagination does the rest by combining reality with dreams and hopes. Through this mental process men develop a different time perspective, tinged perhaps with a Spanish philosophy of life, no longer thinking of the past as something remote and forgotten but recalling it as something that happened only yesterday. There is little or no projection into the future in this outlook of time; people who acquire this mental attitude advance with their backs to the future, living in a past that is not unreal because it never quite ceased to exist.

This ideal medium for the cultivation of legendary lore is further strengthened by those historical events that serve as

Oñate that they had diggings at several points in the Southwest. Herbert Eugene Bolton, *Spanish Exploration in the Southwest, 1542–1706*, 238, gives a translation of an "Account of the Discovery of the Mines, 1599." The assay ordered by Oñate of the ore samples brought back by Marcos Farfán de los Godos showed a silver content of eleven ounces to the quintal.

touchstones to memory, and act as triggers to the imagination. The first legend of the Southwest begins for Europeans when Álvar Núñez Cabeza de Vaca saw an Indian give a *cascabel de cobre,* a copper rattle, to one of his companions. This simple happening combined with the tales he had heard about gold-paved cities created the legend of Quivira. A few years later, Fray Marcos may have seen the walls of Hawikuh at sunset before he returned to Mexico, or thought he saw them, and added to the story believed by those who followed in his footsteps, as follow they did. Stories continued to circulate and accumulate, not only of cities paved with gold but of mountains of solid ore and lakes shimmering with quicksilver.

There was no follow-up of these later tales after the disillusionment of Quivira, but some writers claim that the legend of Cerro Azul[4] was in the back of Oñate's mind when he sent some of his expeditions westward from Santa Fe to find the sea. In 1692, however, the story of this fabulous mountain not only reached the ears of Diego de Vargas but also those of the Viceroy who sent for specimens of a substance thought to be quicksilver. Some historians go so far as to suggest that the legend of Cerro Azul was the primary reason for the reconquest of New Mexico by Diego de Vargas in 1692. There had been considerable correspondence and conversation about the feasibility of developing mining operations in what is now western New Mexico provided the province of "the Kingdom of New Mexico" were first reconquered.

Just a few years after the reconquest, a factual account of a rich deposit was reported by two fugitives from justice, who

[4] The legend of Cerro Azul or Sierra Azul seems to have persisted through the reconquest by de Vargas in 1692. In 1689 when Toribio de Huerta was applying to the king for authority to undertake the reconquest, he "reminded the monarch that between Zuñi and Moqui was the Sierra Azul, a region immensely rich in silver. . . ." *See* Hubert Howe Bancroft, *History of Arizona and New Mexico,* 195.

while hiding in the mountains near Chihuahua City, came across an incredibly rich lode in 1700. Tradition weaves its thread around the story saying that the two outlaws traded their secret for a pardon given them by the Bishop of Durango. The churchman added the proviso that 2 per cent of the returns from the mines be used to build the cathedral of Chihuahua. The gold rush that followed this discovery developed into the "Real de Santa Eulalia," where hundreds of millions of dollars' worth of silver have been mined and continue to be mined to the present day.

Hardly had the incident of Santa Eulalia been forgotten when the river at Batopilas in northern Sonora rose to an unprecedented level and its widened channel uncovered a bare rock, which turned out to be solid silver. The mine was named "La Nevada" and some of the enormous specimens of virgin silver were sent not only to the Viceroy in Mexico City but to the royal court in Madrid. Apparently this was no flash in the pan operation, according to Don Martín Salido, who quotes a nineteenth century record saying that the royal fifth that reached the coffers of the king amounted to an equivalent of thirty million dollars. Eventually the whole Chihuahua district brought in over five hundred producing mines.

In 1736 the discovery of Santa Eulalia and the lucky find of Batopilas were obscured, for a short time at least, by the finding near the Pima village of Arizona of a fantastic surface nugget of pure silver weighing twenty-seven hundred pounds. The location of "Bolas de Plata," as the site was named, is attributed to a Yaqui Indian who showed a Mexican friend a spot where silver seemed to grow right out of the ground. The first nugget was followed by two lesser ones weighing four hundred and two hundred pounds respectively. The total combined weight of the three nuggets was one ton and thirteen hundred pounds. The event attained such significance that eventually the Indian fighter, Don Juan Bautista de Anza, the Viceroy of Mexico, the Royal Fiscal, and King Philip V himself became involved in the affair. Before it was settled, King Philip issued a decree from Aranjuez on May 28, 1741, terminating the prosecution instituted against Don Domingo Asmendi for non-payment of duties to the royal treasury for this very silver.

This *criadero de plata*, literally a place where silver grew out of the ground, was rediscovered in 1854 by a party of twelve Americans led by Charles Schuchard,[5] who found on the surface a lump of silver weighing nineteen pounds. The land was still in uncertain status as a result of the war with Mexico, but when the Gadsden Purchase was consummated Schuchard and another man named Blanding established the Arizona Exploring and Mining Company where the city of Ajo now stands. This name is supposed to have influenced the choice of name for the territory when it was established. The Spaniards had called it Arizonac from the two Pima words, *ari,* meaning "few," and *zoni* meaning "springs." Whether from the Spanish "Arizonac" or from the Pima dialect, this semiarid state is aptly named "Few Springs" or "Arizona."

Nothing like the enormous nuggets of Arizona has been found lately in the Southwest, although treasure-hunters speak of "stacks of gold worth twenty-two million dollars." Once in a while, however, someone gets a thrill such as the one experienced by the New Mexico farm hand who in 1916 found an old Spanish chest hidden in a cave in the Ladrones Mountains.[6] The very name of the place is suggestive of hoarded gold and

[5] When Schuchard rediscovered the place where the Bolas de Plata were found, he was driven away by Mexicans who claimed rightfully that it was Mexican territory. *See* Thomas Ashton Rickard, *A History of American Mining.*

[6] Ladrones Mountains is a cluster of rugged crags rising to a height of 9,185 feet just west of Highway 85 about sixty miles south of Albuquerque. The official name for these mountains is Sierra Ladrones; it was already in use in 1692.

hidden treasure: "Thieves Mountains!" It is a well established fact that many a highwayman took refuge in these rugged peaks north of Socorro, New Mexico, after assaulting a pack train or holding up the stagecoach on the Camino Real.

The chest along with its unexpected contents is now owned by Edgar J. Goodspeed of Chicago. It must have been somewhat of a disappointment for the finder not to see it filled with doubloons. Instead, he found six old books, all published before 1600. One was a folio of the New Testament in Greek, dated 1596; another was a Hebrew Bible published in 1584 in Antwerp, and once the property of the Barefoot Augustinians of Valladolid, Spain. The oldest book was a collection of medieval sermons dated 1531, and the rest were works of Latin authors such as Quintilian. It is pretty well accepted today that these books were the property of a missionary named Fray Diego Jimenez who worked in northern Mexico between 1632 and 1678. Dr. Goodspeed, who reported the find in *El Palacio* on June 1, 1922, conjectures that the chest had been taken by thieves along the Spanish Trail thinking it contained something besides books, or that if it did contain something of more practical value to the robbers, they disposed of that and left what obviously did not interest them.

Accidental finds are usually the more remarkable because the finder has no preconceived notion of what he runs into. A prospector who locates a vein is elated at his success, but not really very surprised because that is what he was looking for. But when a prospector is not even prospecting and runs into a treasure then it is more surprising. Such was the case of Ben Brown in southern New Mexico. He was well acquainted with the Southwest, but at the time when he went out to find a deer he was not particularly interested in a treasure other than venison for his camp.

CHAPTER 4

The treasure of "El Chato" Nevárez

◆

Late in the fall of 1913 Ben Brown left his prospector's camp one afternoon to look for a deer along the foothills below the Organ Mountains. Toward the end of the day he came upon a good-sized mule deer buck as he reached the top of a ravine, but before he could get him in the sights of his Winchester the deer bounded gracefully and disappeared in the arroyo below him. The buck was not entirely unharmed because Ben Brown's quick shot from the hip had caught him in the shanks, as the trail of blood indicated. Confident that the wound would slow the critter down, Ben followed the trail over the scrub-covered arroyos and through the thick chamiso expecting to find him lying somewhere along the trail. Apparently the deer was not badly wounded; he outdistanced the young prospector by keeping constantly under cover and always out of range until he disappeared. Tired and disappointed by his long and unsuccessful hunt, Ben Brown threw himself down at the foot of a gnarled juniper standing on the brow of the first hill he came to.

As he sat listening to his own breathing, Ben's eyes glanced over the landscape hoping to see something move, anything that would make a meal for a hungry mining man. Gradually his gaze shifted to the ground where he was sitting, and before long his prospecting eye caught a peculiarity about the hillside, which

36

at first glance had not been apparent. He got to his feet and began a closer inspection of the terrain; something about it intrigued him. In a few minutes it became quite clear that the place where he had been sitting was a fill-in of some sort. The question that arose in his mind was why anyone would bother to fill a depression of a hill so far away from nowhere, but if it was a fill-in, what was it hiding?

Still on his feet he began to scan the horizon to get his bearings, and when he turned his face eastward he paused to take a second and more careful look; he had made a startling discovery. Three conical peaks leading toward the mountain range behind them stood out in perfect array. He leaned his gun against the juniper and started walking toward the rising sun—"One, two, three..." and on, until he reached two hundred fifty. He stopped, looked back, and put together a pile of rocks, then turned north and began counting the same number of paces. He had reached the top of another rise from which he could see straight ahead into the Jornada del Muerto.[1] He went back to the tree and walked down the arroyo counting one hundred paces. There was no spring visible, but when he scraped the surface with his toe he noticed that the sand was moist.

Ben Brown felt sure that he had accidentally stumbled upon the location of a treasure he had learned about from a convict, a member of a gang working under him during the building of the road between Hot Springs and Socorro. He had never thought of searching for it, but the depression of that hill, the three conical

[1] Arduous though travel was through the Jornada del Muerto, so named because of the number of people who perished while crossing it, it was regularly used because it was a convenient short-cut. The Spanish Trail, which followed the Río Grande north most of the way, left it at Robledo just north of the modern city of Las Cruces and did not rejoin it until about ninety miles north at Fray Cristobal. The Río Grande swings on an arc to the west and the Jornada is a straight line. Oñate, the first colonizer of New Mexico, used it when he brought his settlers in 1598.

peaks, and the faint trace of water from what may have been the "dripping spring" the convict gave as the third landmark, was enough to persuade him that he had run into the hiding place of "El Chato's Treasure."

El Chato was a renegade who held out in the mountains from Tortugas Peak north to the Caballo Range, harrying the traffic of the Camino Real and assaulting the pack trains loaded with cargo coming up from Chihuahua. His specialty was the *conductas*[2] with little or no military escort, and any time valuables were being transported El Chato could be expected to attack from his hideout in the mountains east of the Río Grande in southern New Mexico. He had earned the name of "El Chato," meaning "Pug-nose," in an encounter with a Spanish cavalryman who had come close to ending his career with a sabre blow. Between 1639 and 1649,[3] he terrorized the countryside along the Mesilla Valley, and with his band of cutthroats defied the scant protection which the Spanish government sent beyond El Paso del Norte. According to tradition, his hideout was in Soledad Canyon in the rugged Organ Mountains, but no one had dared to follow him to his lair.

The best haul on record made by El Chato came toward the end of his depredations, and probably was the last one he ever made. He chose for his victims a band of missionaries coming up the Spanish Trail with an *atajo* of pack mules loaded with

[2] *See* Cleve Hallenbeck, *Land of the Conquistadores*, 303. This author states that the trading caravans from New Mexico converged from places as far north as Taos at an established location and then proceeded on their way to the Chihuahua Fair. He gives the following statistics: "*Conductas* left in November, rendevouzed in Sevillita of La Jolla, arrived in Chihuahua in January. There were as many as 300 wagons, 600 mules, 400 horses. Women and children. They used the boleta in trade."

[3] The dates given in the El Chato story do not accord with the historical conditions at that time. There was, for example, no presidio at El Paso until after 1680. The discrepancy is typical of the manner in which traditions develop.

church property and other valuables they were bringing from
Mexico City. They had begun their journey in Acólmán,[4] a
monastery thirty-nine miles northeast of Mexico City founded

[4] The publication of José Montes de Oca, *San Agustín de Acólmán*, gives
an up-to-date account of the old monastery from its founding to the present
time. On the reproduction of the monastery's north facade there is this interesting legend: "Acabose esta obra año de 1560 reinando el Rey Don Felipe

by Fray Andrés de Olmos in 1524 and later modified and enlarged by the Augustinian monks. El Chato learned through
his grapevine that these monks were not bringing an ordinary
cargo of church supplies, but that they had with them an assortment of golden chandeliers, baptismal urns, chalices, and no
small amount of coined silver.

Toward the close of the day, in the spring of 1649, the caravan of pack mules and robed friars reached the foothills below
the Organ Mountains and expected to make Robledo before
nightfall, the place where travelers rested their animals and prepared for the ordeal of the grueling Jornada del Muerto. Suddenly, from the recesses of the mountains emerged a band of
ruffians riding at full gallop into the group of startled and tired
monks. The pack mules, excited by the sudden apparition, scattered over the hillsides, but the men drove them with their lati-
gos back towards the mountains away from the trail and their
rightful owners. Some of the churchmen tried to hold to the
halters of their pack animals, but the relentless outlaws whacked
the *reatas* with their knives and drove the entire *atajo* out of
sight into the mountain fastness.

It was indeed a sad group of missionaries who walked back
to the presidio[5] of El Paso del Norte three days later to report
the daring daylight attack of El Chato. The small garrison had
to wait until reinforcements were sent for to Durango, and as
soon as the troops arrived they were augmented by volunteers

---

nuestro Señor, Hijo del Emperador Carlos V, y gobernando esta Nueva España
su II virrey, don Luis Velasco con cuyo favor se edificó."

[5] There were three designations used in colonial days for settlements of
various sizes. The large cities usually had an *"ayuntamiento"* and the smaller
towns, a *cabildo;* but out on the frontier of the empire there were garrisons
with nothing more than soldiers and sometimes a missionary or two. These
were called *presidios,* and El Paso as one of the northernmost frontier govern-
ments went by that name for a long time. There are still towns in both California and Texas that have retained the name "presidio."

who had personal accounts to settle with the infamous cutthroat. These soldiers were disguised as travelers. El Chato and his men, lured from their hideout by this device, attacked them, and in the battle that followed, every member of his band was either killed, fatally wounded, or captured. El Chato himself, whose real name was Pedro Nevárez, was taken prisoner and sent under guard to Mexico City where he was tried and hanged. Some accounts say that before he died he tried to make amends for his sins by giving a map of his cache in the Organ Mountains, while other versions say that he was tight-lipped to the end.

Probably nothing would ever have been known about the treasure of the famous outlaw had the Apache Chief Victorio[6] not attacked the mission church in Doña Ana. After tearing down and burning all they could find, the Indians scattered papers, books, and correspondence over the mesa on the way out of the village. Some of the church records made interesting reading, but nothing caused so much comment as a copy of a letter some priest had written to the monastery of Acólmán back in the seventeenth century. According to this letter, one of El Chato's badly wounded men had dragged himself to the priest's quarters somewhere in the valley the night after the attack and before dying gave a complete description of his accomplices as well as the location of the hoard in the nearby mountains. The priest conveyed this information by letter to the church authorities in Mexico City but kept a copy for his own records. The part of the document, which has appeared in many versions is the following:

In Soledad Canyon there is a natural cave on the brow of a hill opening toward the south. There is a cross cut into the rock above the entrance of the cave and directly in front of a young juniper tree. For better directions, (*para mejores señas*) there are three medium sized peaks toward the rising sun whose shadows converge in the morning 250 paces east of the cave's entrance and a little to the south. Two hundred and fifty paces from this point directly north you will come to a promontory, a *loma,* from where by looking straight ahead you can see the Jornada del Muerto, as far as the eye can see. The distance from this point back to the cave should be exactly the same as the distance to the place where the shadows converge. One hundred

[6] Chief Victorio was a Chiricahua Apache, who left the reservation in 1877, and went on the warpath with his two principal lieutenants, Loco and Nana. He spread terror throughout southern New Mexico and Arizona until 1881, when he was attacked and killed by Mexican troops in Chihuahua. He was succeeded as a raider by the well-known Geronimo.

paces from the entrance of the cave down to the nearby arroyo, and in line with the point of convergence, you will find a dripping spring.

The entrance to the cave has been covered to a depth of a man's height, (*un estado*) and ten *varas* beyond the entrance of it there is an adobe wall which must be taken down. At the bottom of a long tunnel, the cave separates into two parts: the left cave contains coined silver, more than two *atajos* can carry, the right cave contains golden chandeliers, urns, crucifixes, gold images and monstrances of beaten gold.

Eventually the story of the dying outlaw's confession reached the ears of treasure-hunters as far east as New York. They arrived in Las Cruces, New Mexico, seeking guides to take them into the mountains. The local residents too were not idle; some set off small dynamite charges in the belief that the detonation would echo wherever there was a cave or would cause a landslide that would lay bare the opening to the treasure. Many attempts ended in disappointment and even discomfort to the treasure hunters. Will Douthitt and his partner Lewis from Estancia, New Mexico, claimed to have found a document in a church in Mexico City in the early twenties with which they located a cave certain to be that of El Chato. They reported to the sheriff of Torrance County that when they were returning from the cave with two gold bars taken from a "cord" stacked inside, they were waylaid by a band of masked men who, tortured them with hot wires and forced them to give up the gold they were carrying. Back in Estancia they tried to get Governor Dillon to send a detachment of the National Guard stationed in the village at that time to protect them, but when he refused they went back alone and were once more intercepted by the band of masked men and robbed.

Ben Brown, the prospector working a claim near the Organ Mountains, never reported anything so simple as walking into a cave and coming out loaded with gold bars. The version he had learned from the convict on the chain gang got considerable support when Prof. George Sánchez of the University of Texas was shown a manuscript at a convention in Tempe, Arizona, by one of the professors attending the meeting. This man, whose name I was never able to run down after a year of correspondence, had a brother in El Paso who worked in a shop where they repaired ancient and outmoded strong boxes. One day while removing the worn interior wall of a Spanish safe, they came across a manuscript that someone had placed between the inner lining and the steel wall. According to the repairman in El Paso, the strongbox had originally come from the Acólmán monastery, and had been brought to the shop for repair.

I tried to follow up the trail of this letter, but by the time I got to it Pearl Harbor was attacked and the investigation was suspended while I spent the next three years in the Air Corps. At the close of the war, I took up the trail again but by that time no one remembered the name of the informant and many of those who had attended the meeting in Tempe were dead.

The interesting point about the letter taken from the strongbox was that it complemented the version of the dying outlaw's confession that Ben Brown knew and was guided by when he made his original discovery. This was based on the tradition that El Chato had decided when he felt the noose tightening around his neck to expiate his sins and tell where he had buried his ill-gotten treasure. Several copies of this confession have appeared in various places at different times, and this proliferation has led to the conjecture that the sacristan of the priest in Mexico who officiated at the hanging of El Chato made copies for his friends, and may have even profited by selling them. One of these documents is filed in the library of the New Mexico Museum in Santa Fe with the date of February 10, 1650. Another version was published by Otto Goetz in the March, 1940, issue of the *New Mexico*

Magazine. All of these confessions are supposedly written in Acólmán's Convento de San Agustín. In some of the versions the sacristan signs himself "Vicente Vasques," but in the one given below, the copyist adds the following statement:

> This is a copy taken from the original by the Sacristan of the Convent of San Agustín of the City of Mexico, Bicente Basones, 10th of January, 1861.

This *derrotero* was not the one that Ben Brown used as a guide, but the confession made by El Chato before his execution.

City of Mexico. Convent of San Agustín. April 5, 1650. Guide which Pedro Nevárez, alias 'El Chato' left on his death.

Ask at El Paso del Norte for the Organ Mountains which are along the river to the right. It's about two days on horseback at a good rate, and the sierra is somewhat scattered, topped with some crested peaks. You will find two Passes, Tortugas and Soledad, covered with numerous junipers. Before reaching the first Pass, go halfway up the mountain until you come to a thick cedar. Measure 100 *varas* straight down to a blue flagstone marked with a large cross. Remove this rock and dig to a depth of an *estado* and there you will find six *atajos* of silver bars.

Return to Soledad Pass and follow the trail to the spring which runs toward the meadow. It is overgrown with cattails. Continue along the slope of the mountain and look for three large cedars standing wide apart. Directly in front of these are three flat rocks and between them and the cedars is covered the mine of the Spaniard Jorge Colon. The flat rocks can be distinguished by a large cross cut with a crowbar.

The opening to the mine, which is so rich that you can cut the solid silver from the vein, is covered with heavy timbers and a red rock moved on top of it by 25 men using levers. You may be able to see part of the opening by removing the dirt and the gravel on top. You can also notice the marks on the rock made by the crowbars.

As you enter the mine you will find a large number of beaten gold images, chandeliers, crosses, vases, platters, monstrances, crucifixes and many things of gold and silver. After removing all this, go down the ladder where you will find large stacks of silver bars and mining implements. As a further sign, as you walk toward the first mountain Pass of which I speak, you will notice a draw or deep hollow. The treasures are located on either side, one toward the rising sun and the other toward the setting sun.

Although Ben Brown knew nothing of this map, his information and the written account had a number of points in common: the spring, the cross cut on the rock, and *Soledad* applying to either peak or canyon. Either story mentioned enough buried treasure to entice the most cynical treasure-hunter, and for a man like Ben Brown who had dug himself into mountains with much less to go on, the spot by the juniper tree in the barren hills of southern New Mexico was good enough for a try.

Early in the morning after his initial discovery, Ben Brown arrived with a pick and shovel, eager to begin digging as soon as the converging shadows of the three peaks verified the location. He did not have long to wait; as the sun rose higher the gaps between the shadows cast by the *picachos* began to close until they formed a single unmistakable shadow on the hillside. In his excitement, Ben wanted to clear out the entire depression, but when he realized the size of the project he did some close figuring and decided to cut a shaft straight down against the hillside where the opening of the cave should be. By midmorning he had dug his own height into a square hole wide enough to give him elbow room, and was about to sit down to catch his breath when his shovel bit into solid rock. Ben Brown forgot how tired he was; he cleared away the loose filling around a flat, smooth rock running perpendicularly into the shaft he was digging, and uncovered the most important clue: a roughly hewn cross, cut deeply into the face of the rock. It was no freak of nature; the chisel marks were clearly visible when he rubbed off the soil that stuck to the grooves.

A very tired, but very excited prospector sat down at the bottom of the pit to roll a cigarette and turn over in his mind the first day's findings. The more he thought it over the more convinced he became that he was on the right trail. When would he find the cave? That would have to wait until the following day. Just now he had other things to attend to. He covered the face of the rock, climbed out, and headed back to his mining claim in the nearby Organ Mountains.

Ben Brown was up early the next morning; it was moving day for him. The tent, bed-roll, and tools were loaded into an ancient automobile to which he affectionately referred years later as his "wobble–knee" when the knee-action type of wheel suspension was put on the market. He drove to Las Cruces and stopped at a grocery store and also at the country clerk's office to register a new claim. His next problem was to find a trail for his car back to the new campsite through the dry arroyo beds and the chamiso-covered mesas. The old "wobble–knee" chugged, strained, and steamed over the rough terrain and broke a new path over the crust of dry sand until it reached the dead end of an arroyo just below the hill where he had been digging the night before.

He carried his gear and supplies to the foot of his now familiar juniper tree, and as soon as his tent was up he proceeded to set up the monuments for his new claim. In one of these he concealed an empty tobacco can with an official sheet of paper stating that Ben Brown of Doña Ana County was now working this "mining claim."

The cross on the rock marked the mouth of a cave, but not an open cave. Before Ben could enter he had to clear away the muck and topsoil with which it had been sealed for centuries. There were tons of loose earth to move out and the treasure-hunter began to wonder why El Chato and his brigands had taken so much trouble to conceal their loot. Each shovelful had to be relayed from the cave to the shaft and then to the surface. While moving the fill to the surface Ben found a copper coin, a Spanish *cuarto,* with the date 1635 on one side and a sovereign's profile on the other. It was clear to him that someone had been there long before him. Days later he came to the adobe wall the directions told about. It too came down with a crowbar. Beyond it on a shelf was the dry skeleton of a lizard, which disintegrated at the touch of his hand, but the most encouraging sign was a small tool about a foot long with a pick on one side and a hatchet blade on the other, a miner's tool made of Spanish hand-forged steel.[7]

A short distance beyond the adobe wall, the cave dropped down to a forty-five degree angle and narrowed to the point where the earth had to be taken out a bucketful at a time. Ben would go down, drag himself back on his belly where he could stand upright, and empty each bucket on the surface. It was tedious and slow, but he kept it up the first year until bad weather and an empty larder forced him to leave.

Another grubstake was not easy to lay aside for a man with two little girls to support, and so Ben Brown found a place up in the Magdalena Mountains at the ranger station in Water Canyon. He panned enough gold in the creek back of the cabin to keep him and his girls going. During weekends he played the fiddle at country dances, and the hunting season provided him with a little cash from hunters who could profit by his knowledge of the outdoors. For several years he alternated all these varied activities, going down to the Organ Mountains whenever

[7] When Prospector Ben Brown found the mining tool in the cave, he sent it to the Field Museum in Chicago for identification. He was told that it was hand-forged Spanish steel.

48

he got a little ahead, to clear out more muck and get closer to the treasure.

In the fall of 1934 while hunting in the Magdalena Mountains, I came across Ben Brown, now a middle-aged man with a greying stubble of beard and a mischievous squint to his blue eyes. We hunted together for three days, got our deer, and went down to his cabin to try some of the venison chili con carne he had been telling me about. We spent most of the night swapping tales about the country and getting better acquainted. Ben asked me if I could get him a copy of J. Frank Dobie's *Coronado's Children;* he had heard it contained some awfully good yarns. The next time I was in Austin I told Frank about Ben Brown and together we inscribed a copy of his book "To Ben Brown, the prospector of Water Canyon."

The following season I went directly to Ben's cabin. Early the morning after I arrived we walked up Seven Mile Canyon to the top of Old Baldy, where we sat down to eat lunch and swap a few more tales about the country. Ben had enjoyed Dobie's book immensely, but there was one story he had not found in it.

"Have you ever heard about El Chato's treasure down by Las Cruces?" he asked.

I told him the version of the story I knew, and he listened attentively to the end.

"That's the story all right, but you've got the location wrong. Most people do; they think that Soledad Canyon is in the Organ Mountains and that ain't right. The name of the canyon is the same, but it's in another range of mountains. That's the reason nobody has even come close to the treasure."

It was my turn to listen. He told me the story I have just related, and at the end surprised me by asking if I wanted to take a look at the cave.

49

"Come some weekend and we'll drive down and see what it's like. Don't mention it to anybody; you come down by yourself."

The following spring we drove down to Las Cruces, where I spent the most sleepless night of my life at a hotel, and early the next morning we back-tracked to the village of Doña Ana. From the highway we turned east, drove under a railroad trestle through an arroyo and followed the winding bed toward the foothills over a blurred trail until we came to the end at the foot of a steep hill.

"We'll have to walk the rest of the way. It ain't far," said Ben.

When we had gone up the hill a way, he stopped and pointed to what looked like the tailings of a mine shaft. I asked him about the juniper that was supposed to be at the entrance of the cave.

"I cut it down the second day. People might use it for a landmark and come snooping around."

The shaft had been enlarged in order to accommodate a hand winch Ben was using to lift the fill-in to the surface. We went down a ladder to the entrance of the cave; it was the size of a small room.

"Well, this is it. Shall we go in and look around?"

We did. The tunnel against the hillside had the appearance of a natural cave, very similar to the subterranean formations extending east to the well-known Carlsbad Caverns, except that there was no moisture and the floor was covered with topsoil. For a short distance we walked upright; then we stooped, and finally began crawling on all fours. About two hundred feet down into the earth we came to a point where the cave split into a Y going in two directions. I took one side and Ben followed along the other. This was as far as he had cleared. The fill-in made it difficult to move, even though I was now dragging myself on my belly. Finally I reached a place where the rocks on the cave floor would permit no further progress. By the beam of a five-cell flashlight I could see that the opening continued indefinitely, and by bathing the walls and ceiling ahead with light I was able to take a few time exposures with my camera.

Satisfied that I had gone as far as I could, I started to back out and found myself tightly wedged in the narrow opening. My efforts to dislodge myself uphill raised so much dust that I found it difficult to breathe, and so I lay still until the dust settled down and I gathered myself together. I knew Ben was on the other spur of the cave but there was so much earth between us that my cries for him could not be heard. After a very long wait during which I had an opportunity to review most of my past life, it was reassuring to feel Ben's hands gripping my ankles. The opening was large enough for him but not for a person fifty pounds heavier.

When we got back to the surface and had cleared our lungs of the dry dust of the cave, Ben pointed out the landmarks of the three peaks, showed me the dreaded Jornada, and led me down to another hole he had cleared out down the arroyo. At the bottom was a cement drinking trough filled with water seeping from the wet sand around it. According to Ben, the travelers on the old Spanish Trail watered their stock at this point just before starting the dry trek across the desert.

On the way back to Magdalena, Ben was trying to formulate a plan whereby he could get power machinery to finish cleaning out the cave. The only solution was to find someone in Albuquerque interested in such an enterprise on a share basis.

There was an elderly lawyer by the name of John Baron Burg, who had married into the well-known Spanish family of Otero, and who still had some of the pioneer spirit of adventure.

He agreed to finance the whole operation on condition that he retain possession of the dig to exploit as a tourist attraction in case nothing was found. Ben was willing to go along with this stipulation; and so the three of us drove down to the cave again. Just about the time we were to begin the formal deal, the Taylor Act was passed by Congress, and under this legislation the lawyer said he could not acquire possession of the property. Thus the arrangement fell through.

Except for an occasional trip to keep his claim active, Ben made very little progress during the depression years; but he continued to nurse the hope that when one of his other claims in Water Canyon came through he would have enough funds to dig the treasure he was sure lay at the bottom of the cave.

"I ain't given up yit! Look at this mining tool and at this coin. How did they get there into that hole? Someone was down there before me and for a very good reason. Some day I'll find out."

He had not found out by the time World War II broke out, but he found out that a tungsten claim he had in the canyon and another small mine he called "The Little Pittsburg" was salable. This left him free to roam around the mountains and continue his prospecting. On his way to Socorro he stopped a few miles below the entrance to Water Canyon and spent the afternoon walking over the hills south of the highway. Among the specimens he brought back to the car was a rock with traces of perlite. He had heard that there was a market for this mineral, and so he sent some samples to be tested in Denver. When he got his report he staked out the whole hillside where he had picked up the specimen and began a new type of mining.

Upon my return from Europe at the end of World War II, I drove down to Water Canyon to look up my old friend, and to my great surprise found him living in a cabin with a brand new roof and with a shiny automobile parked in his front yard under the pine trees. As I drove up to the front door, a bald-headed man, hardy and spry from outdoor living, walked out out of the cabin.

"Do you know if an old gopher by the name of Ben Brown is still roaming around these hills?" I asked.

With his accustomed grin and squint he answered, "He is, so fur as I know. The sheriff ain't caught up with him yit."

We went into the cabin where Ben poured the usual cup of coffee for me and one for himself out of a shiny percolator! Around the room I noticed running water, a sink, a new stove, and an electric refrigerator.

"Well, Ben, it looks as though you finally dug up El Chato!"

"No, not yit. I found another one right in my back yard. Did you notice that big plant down the road a ways?"

It was the property of the Great Lakes Carbon Corporation, a processing plant working a claim that Ben had sold to that company during the war. The income tax he had paid after the sale was greater than his earnings during all the years he had been prospecting.

Eventually we got around to the cave in Doña Ana County when I spied the Spanish forged steel tool lying on a shelf.

"It's still there, but I've got something better cooking. Come over during the hunting season and we'll talk about it. We can drive down there any time you're free. I'll drive my car this time."

Ben Brown is no longer worried about funds. He started chasing a wounded deer one afternoon, ran into a treasure site, and later struck a fortune in his back yard. He is still waiting for another pot of gold at the end of an arroyo in southern New Mexico. The last letter I received from Ben added an interesting note:

I could tell you a lot more if I could talk to you, but I can hardly write so you can read it. My spelling is very bad but maybe you can figure it out some way. Best of luck to you. As ever, your friend,

BEN BROWN.

CHAPTER 5

THE GOLD ON SMELTER HILL

◆

THE RÍO GRANDE runs from north to south across the entire
state of New Mexico, but at El Paso, Texas, it turns southeast
between the Franklin Mountains on the north and the Mexican
Sierras on the south, creating the international boundary between
the United States and Mexico along the state of Texas. History, romance, and fortune as well as tragedy summon up re-
membrances of things past at the very mention of this seven-
teen-hundred-mile river for those who have lived near it. The
largest city along the Río Grande is El Paso, a city that grew
from the villages of the Mansos Indians and the mission of Nuestra Señora de Guadalupe de los Mansos back in the seventeenth
century; and the original village got its name from the mountain pass through which the river runs. El Paso is unique, neither
Mexican, nor Texan, nor New Mexican, and yet it is all three.
Into its personality are woven the traditions of the Indians, the
Spanish conquerors, the Anglo traders, the miners, and the
cattlemen, as well as the present day Mexicans and New Mexicans. Most Texans will tell you that it is not part of Texas, and
the New Mexicans hardly claim the old city despite the fact that
all of them had to go through the "Pass city" to get to whatever
settlement they were going to in colonial days. Mexico has contributed a good half of its population but El Paso is still *"El otro*

lado," the other side, to the residents across the river in Juárez. So the old city nestled in the farthest corner of Texas remains the crucible of three cultures, Spanish, Anglo, and Indian, a mixture of the races that developed and today inhabit the New World.

Fortunato Sálaz was born down the valley not very far from El Paso, and like so many of the old residents in that part of the country, he knew little about his ancestors except that they had always lived in the vicinity, either north or south of the city according to the fortunes of the family. Just now, Fortunato was living north of El Paso at the settlement of "La Esmelda," which is the nearest phonetic rendering of the English "Smelter." He didn't actually live at the smelter village, for he wasn't employed by the smelter; he was staying at a camp a few hundred yards beyond the plant, where the Southern Pacific Railroad was putting a bridge across the Río Grande to join the line to California. He was a member of a crew employed to dig with pick and shovel before the advent of power machinery in the early eighties. Fresnos and horse-drawn scrapers moved the earth loosened by large plows, and the men did the finishing work with spades and shovels. Fortunato was accustomed to the drudgery of backbreaking work and did not mind the ten long hours he put in every day along with hundreds of his compañeros.

The one thing that Fortunato did mind, and objected to in his passive manner, was the long evenings at camp. The working gangs were quartered in tents where they did their cooking and sleeping. After wolfing down the evening meal they soon forgot how tired they were and sat around in the tents talking and singing, and when there was tequila in camp, being a bit too rowdy for the quiet and retiring Fortunato. He didn't play cards, didn't know how, he said to those who invited him to join a table, and was too bashful to try to sing. What he most wanted was to lie back on his bed-roll and get a good night's sleep, but there was little chance to do this early in the evening when his compañeros were going strong with their simple and loud merrymaking.

All through the week he put up with the noisy chatter by rolling himself as far away into a corner of the tent as he could, but on Saturdays and Sundays things were different. Most of the men from the hillside camp drove or caught rides in wagons going to El Paso and to Juárez where they could see a bullfight on Sunday afternoon. Those who had families took their earnings home to pay for the grocery bill and visit with their loved ones, but Fortunato was alone and preferred to remain at camp resting or visiting quietly with those who stayed behind. Sometimes he would take a walk farther up the hill toward Mount Franklin where he could enjoy the view of the river below him. On one of these solitary weekends, he decided to walk around the hill south of the railroad camp instead of climbing toward the mountain. The smelter was there; he could see the tops of the stacks belching smoke all day long, but had never seen the plant. He decided to see it. He started early one Sunday morning after breakfast and followed a well worn path along the hillside. From time to time he looked back at the camp and watched it slowly disappear as he rounded the side of the hill, until eventually it was out of sight completely.

So intent was he on reaching the plant that he had not noticed he was approaching a small adobe house up the hill from the path he was following; but when he did see it he left the path, following his first impulse, and walked up to it out of simple curiosity, since he had nothing to do and Sunday was a long day. Probably an abandoned house, he thought at first, as he approached the one-room structure; there was no sign of life around it. As he reached the front door he paused and was about to walk in, when in the shaded interior he noticed an old man sitting at a table, his head bent down over a book he was apparently reading. As Fortunato's figure was silhouetted in the doorway, the old man raised his head and for a moment two equally surprised men looked at each other without saying a word. The old man was the first to speak in a well modulated, soft voice.

"*Buenos días,*" said he in Spanish.

The friendly greeting put Fortunato at ease and helped him to decide what to do as he stood for an instant at the entrance. He returned the greeting and was about to continue on his way when the same soft voice invited him to come in.

"Come in. Are you a *forastero,* a stranger in these parts, or are you a traveler?" the old man inquired.

Fortunato found his tongue and explained that he was out for a walk and had decided to look at the smelter, but that when he saw the house he was curious to see if it was inhabited. The old man bade the visitor sit down on the other chair by the table, and Fortunato did so mechanically, still astonished to have found the house occupied. He let his eyes wander over the interior and noticed a cot in a corner of the room, a much used small stove with a pipe to the wall, and an improvised cupboard made from stacked wooden boxes next to the stove. This, with the table and chairs completed the furnishings of the house.

After a short while, Fortunato was pleased to find out how easy it was to carry on a conversation with his newly made acquaintance. They made desultory talk at first until they became used to each other, and then Fortunato spoke with more ease than was his custom about the work at camp, his tentmates, and how he spent most of his weekends resting or walking about. In the course of their conversation, the old man felt the ill-concealed loneliness and dislike which Fortunato had for the noisiness and late-hour rowdiness of his companions at camp. The camp-laborer learned from the old man that he lived alone and read for pleasure and to while away the hours. Like Fortunato, he had no family; he had outlived what few relatives he had, and having been on the go, traveling around the world, had never had time to have a family of his own. In short, he was an old bachelor living out his years on the hillside by the Río Grande.

Fortunato's personal history did not encompass much more than that of the old man except that being young he hadn't covered as much territory. The other, whose name was Don Nicasio, a venerable name that fitted his bearded face very appropriately, was from the same colonial stock; and after wandering about from one country to another had returned to spend his last days in the country of his birth.

In order to make the morning more pleasant, Don Nicasio made a fire in the stove where the embers were still alive, removed a lid, and put the coffeepot next to the flame, where it soon came to a boil. He reached for a dipper of cold water from a bucket sitting on an empty box by the stove and dropped part of its contents over the coffee in order to settle it. This was an invitation to stay longer, and also served to bring the two men into a closer relationship. They spent most of the day visiting, and Fortunato completely forgot his original plan to see the smelter until midafternoon, when he arose to go. He mentioned his intent to Don Nicasio rather weakly, like a man who is about to change his mind. The old man waived him back into his chair and insisted that he stay for dinner.

"The bean-pot is full and I baked some bread last night, so there's plenty for a good meal."

Fortunato thought of what would be waiting for him at camp and decided to accept, though with some reluctance, fearing that he was taking food from a poor old man. The beans were fried in rendered, hot fat as is the custom on the border; *frijoles refritos,* they call them or re-fried beans, a very tasty dish. After mopping up with a piece of bread the last of the beans on his plate, Don Nicasio suggested in an offhand manner that Fortunato could spend the night with him, or move into the little one-room adobe if he wanted to. Before Fortunato could accept or refuse this unexpected offer of hospitality, the old man continued:

"As you can see, young man, I have little to offer. I lead a simple life, but I want nothing and I am content with my books, though at times I get a little lonesome. If the company of your friends is too trying, you can move your bed-roll here and share my pot of beans before you go to work. It's only a short walk from here, and to a man of your years that is nothing."

Fortunato could hardly believe that he was being invited to live under the peaceful roof of the kindly old man and for a moment did not answer. He rubbed his chin a couple of times and thought of what the change would mean. He no longer would have to roll up into the corner of the tent trying to shut out the noise or the rowdiness of too many tequilas. He could share expenses with his new mate and give him a hand with some of the house chores. Finally, with the courtesy common to Mexican folk, he smiled and refused the offer saying that he did not want to take advantage of his host's good nature. But the old man insisted, as Fortunato knew he would, and in the end he agreed to move in that very Sunday.

The news of Fortunato's sudden move came as a surprise to his tentmates, and at first they thought he had married a girl from Smelter Town. "You can never tell about these quiet boys. They don't say much but they act quickly," the men said. They finally accepted the change and Fortunato walked back and forth every day except Sunday from the little house on the hillside to camp. Every evening when he returned from work there was a simple but tasty meal waiting for him. Don Nicasio too enjoyed having someone with whom to share his meals instead of eating in solitude. Fortunato enjoyed not having to go back to camp to help prepare the community meal. The only chore he had was keeping the water bucket filled with water from the river.

After the dishes were washed and the table cleared away, Don Nicasio would read aloud from time to time if Fortunato showed an interest in what he was reading. Much of his library consisted of religious books, some of them quite old and not very interesting to the young man, who sometimes listened out of courtesy. What he'd rather listen to was the accounts Don Nicasio occasionally related about his travels in Mexico and South America. He tried to draw the old man into telling more about the fabulous Southland. It didn't take much coaxing, for Don Nicasio enjoyed re-living the days of his youth, as he reconstructed his experiences in the silver mines of Chihuahua and his gold quests in the rich placers of the Napo River of the Ecuadorian jungle.

And so the months passed and the work at the railroad camp progressed toward eventual completion. Meanwhile, Don Nicasio and Fortunato built up a close friendship, which the latter knew would also come to an end when he would be forced to go elsewhere in search of another job. One Saturday evening while they sat at the table eating supper, Don Nicasio said to the younger man:

"Son, how would you like to take a walk toward Mt. Franklin[1] for an outing tomorrow? We could take some food along and be back in time for supper."

The suggestion came as a surprise to Fortunato but as the prospect of a break in their usual Sunday routine appealed to him, he agreed enthusiastically. He had never been to the top of the mountain and besides, the summer heat had abated, mak-

[1] The Franklin Mountains extend from El Paso about twenty-five miles north. The highest peak near El Paso is over 7,100 feet high. The present city of El Paso was known as Franklin when it was nothing more than an outpost. El Paso was the original name of present-day Ciudad Juárez.

ing the outdoors much more attractive for climbing. Only one thought troubled Fortunato as he pondered over the coming tramp; could the old man's legs manage the uneven terrain? He put the question bluntly to Don Nicasio.

"Don't you think the ground is a little rough? You know how it is, or maybe we can take it slowly at the start. What do you think?

The old man smiled and assured him that his old legs had carried him for many years over mountains and terrain much more rugged than the *lomas* they were about to walk to.

"Why, son, this is no expedition; just a Sunday walk."

The affair was settled; they would leave early the following day right after breakfast. The next morning Fortunato awakened to the sound of rattling dishes and the smell of coffee; Don Nicasio had made early preparations for their Sunday walk. Breakfast over, they tidied up the table as was their habit and prepared to leave. Don Nicasio reached behind the door and handed Fortunato a long-handled shovel and took one himself.

"Why do we take shovels along?" asked the young man in surprise.

"You'll see when we get to where we're going," the old man answered with a definiteness of purpose that further puzzled Fortunato. He had learned, however, that when his senior partner decided on something there was no alteration of his plans, and usually he had good reason. The young man accordingly took the shovel and went along behind the house, Don Nicasio leading the way up the hillside toward the Franklin Mountains.

It was surprising to Fortunato how well the old man managed over the uneven terrain. He avoided sharp rises when climbing and knew how to take advantage of stretches that seemed almost level, and he didn't waste his breath by talking. In fact they climbed the first hour in silence; but as they went up a little knoll they came upon a narrow flat mesa where Don Nicasio turned to Fortunato suggesting that they sit down to rest.

They had come up higher than the young man had realized, and from their vantage point could see the cluster of tents, stock corrals, and equipment that comprised the railroad camp. Across the river the west spans of the bridge were also being finished, and in a few weeks the job would be completed. The old man saw all this but was more interested in the landmarks he knew so well. Three days due south on horseback lay the Real de Santa Eulalia, that fabulous silver strike where millions had been mined.

"Have you ever seen the cathedral in Chihuahua, son?"

Fortunato had never been to Chihuahua; he had been only within a ten-mile radius of El Paso.

"It's a beautiful cathedral; large too, and it was built with some of the silver mined in Santa Eulalia. Only a small portion of the silver, of course."

Don Nicasio told his young companion about the mines of Chihuahua, the silver lodes around Ajo, and the rich copper mines of Arizona and Sonora. It was strange to hear so much about mining from an old man who lived the life of a recluse on a hillside. It was not the first time that this thought had coursed through Fortunato's mind. If he knew so much about gold and silver, why didn't he dig some for himself? Oh well, they say that prospectors and miners are fond of dreaming and telling of big strikes, the young man thought, and so he listened and enjoyed the stories without trying to figure things out.

At the end of another rolled cigarette, Don Nicasio slowly arose and said to his *compañero*:

"Come, *ándale,* Fortunato. I want to show you something that will enable you to live in comfort some day when you have a family and I am gone."

63

With a feeling of sudden curiosity at first, mixed with guilt at what he had thought when Don Nicasio talked about gold, Fortunato paused for a moment trying to think of something to say; but before he could frame the sentence in his mind the old man shouldered his shovel and was a few paces ahead. Fortunato understood now why they had brought shovels along and was willing to wait in silence without further questioning until the old man was ready to explain. They slowed their pace as they climbed higher and headed toward a clump of scrub oaks trying valiantly to stay alive on the dry, parched soil. As they went around the stunted trees, they came upon another flat rise hidden behind them. Here Don Nicasio stopped and held to his shovel handle with both hands. It was higher now; they could tell the air was becoming thinner and harder to breathe. Fortunato dropped on his haunches to rest, and balanced himself by holding the shovel between his legs.

"How much farther do we go, Don Nicasio?" he asked. The old man looked down at him and said with a faint smile breaking on his wrinkled lace:

"We're here. Come, we have work to do."

Saying this, he walked over to a flat rock showing through the earth and began to scrape the loose soil around the edges. With the easy, graceful movements of a man who has used a shovel for years, Fortunato joined him, cleaned the surface, and uncovered the uneven edges of a rock the length of a man and about a third as wide. When this part of the operation was finished, he looked at the old man, waiting for the next move.

"I think we can pry it loose if we work together from this side," said Don Nicasio. "Push your shovel down as far as it will go and then we'll pry back."

Fortunato joined the old man, put his weight on the shovel, and slid the blade down behind the rock as instructed. They both pushed down and then with easy, short movements began to test the weight of the rock. It was heavy, but gradually they could see it move, a little at a time. Finally it rose about six inches as the men went down on the shovel handles.

"We've got it," grunted the old man; "now let's slide it sideways."

They were slowly pulling on the strained handles trying to keep the rock off the hole and place it on the side, when one of the shovel handles gave way with a sharp crack. The rock settled back into place, covering an opening that had allowed Fortunato a fleeting glimpse. Two disappointed men stood up and looked at the rock, its outline more distinct now that it had been off its resting place.

"Well, there's little we can do now, son. Mainly I wanted to show you the place in case I should die. I'm getting old and before long I'll be gone. There's enough in this hole to take care of all your needs for the rest of your life."

Fortunato was deeply touched by his benefactor's offer and too confused to make any of the many inquiries that surged to his mind. Where had the cache come from, how long had it been there, and what did it consist of? These were questions he wanted to ask, but just now it didn't seem proper. It would sound as though he were interested only in the wealth that lay beneath the rock. He started to thank the old man for his kindness, but the latter raised his hands deprecatingly:

"Son, it's nothing, *No es nada*. It's simply passing on to you what I cannot use. There's no virtue in giving away what you cannot take with you. I have plenty to keep me for the few years that lie ahead. You'll have this some day, and you're welcome to it; you deserve it."

At the end of his speech, the old man turned to go with a finality that left no doubt in Fortunato's mind about his plans. The two walked down more easily than they had climbed, and halfway to the foot they sat down to eat their lunch. Fortunato's mind kept going back to the episode at the rock. He blamed himself for having broken the shovel handle and tried to reconstruct his efforts. Maybe the old man weakened and shifted some of the weight to him—yes, that could have happened. Anyway, they didn't move it, but maybe it was better this way. He was not supposed to have it until his friend died.

It was inevitable that eventually they would talk about the treasure at the rock, and although Fortunato did not open the subject he was glad when Don Nicasio began to discuss it. The old man was very frank and matter-of-fact. He had always known that some day he would come back to this country, the country of his birth; and so every time he returned from one of his expeditions to the south he converted his gains into gold coins, placed them in leather sacks, and dropped them into the hole he had chosen, where no one except him would ever find them.

So Don Nicasio's tales about the wonders of the southlands were no mere fantasy! The two reached the little adobe on the hillside early in the afternoon and began to prepare supper, but when it was on the table Fortunato was too excited to eat with his accustomed gusto. He had heard a number of tales about lost gold treasures and mines, but he had never imagined that some day he would actually get to dig any of these troves. For the first time in his life he thought about the meaning of his name: Fortunato, fortunate, indeed he was fortunate, more so than he ever dreamed he could be!

And so the days, the weeks, and finally the months passed. The railroad bridge was finished, the spans were locked together, and the rails were put across. Fall was in the air and Fortunato had to look for another job somewhere else. He could have stayed on with the old man on the hillside by the Río Grande, but the thought of waiting around for his benefactor to die was too much like a vulture waiting for his meal.

Shortly after he was laid off from the railroad camp, Fortunato heard that there was plenty of work in California. No longer was he afraid to travel away from the land that had been home all his life. His association with Don Nicasio had made a vicarious traveler out of him, as he listened to the wondrous tales about other countries, tales that he now believed in and knew to be true. He accordingly used some of his savings for a trip to California on the very train that he had helped to put across the Río Grande. He promised to keep in touch with Don Nicasio; he would write often and keep him informed of his progress. Yes, he would let him know in case he was hard up, but he hoped he wouldn't need to. True to his promise, Fortunato wrote laboriously penciled letters to his friend, and he in turn answered them in much more legible writing.

Fortunato stayed on in California. He had found a good job, the weather was to his liking, and the country was much greener than the semidesert country around El Paso. When he wrote to Don Nicasio about an important event in his life, his marriage to a little *pochita* he had found in California, his letter was returned with a cancellation that tersely read: DECEASED, Return to Writer. Several weeks had elapsed; hence it was evident that Don Nicasio had already been laid to rest. There was no use going back just now; and when he should go back he wanted to take his family along. He began saving his money for his return, but every time his savings increased, his family did too and consumed his reserve. The longer he put off the trip, the more lethargic he became about it. He was happy, and like so many of the Mexican folk, he gradually became afflicted by a characteristic wantlessness, which bordered on contentment or was born of it.

One day Fortunato decided on a plan that would get him the treasure without his having to make the trip back to El Paso. He knew a priest who was well versed in such things as treasures and who was also a man of integrity whom he could trust; and so he wrote him a letter giving him all the details of the exact location of the rock he had tried to pry loose one Sunday. The priest, following the instructions, went back to the railroad bridge hoping to retrace the steps of old Nicasio and Fortunato. There was no trace of the camp after these many years and the little adobe hut where the old man had lived had been swallowed up in a housing project. The priest tried to find the knoll, the flat mesa, and the rock without success. Fortune still awaits someone with a stronger shovel handle than the one Fortunato used at the turn of the century.

CHAPTER 6

FATE HAS THE FINAL WORD

◆

DON RAFAEL LUCERO was a robust, eighty-five-year-old New Mexican with the energy of a man half his age and the interest in life of a twenty-year-old. He had picked up enough legal knowledge from an old lawbook in Spanish to plead simple cases in justice of the peace courts in San Miguel County, where he spent most of his time. At the turn of the century he had served under Captain Sena of the Mounted Police, a body of law enforcement officers organized to curb rustlers, whose thieving had become a threat to cattlemen in territorial days. The old man wasn't tall; he was short, broad-chested and thick-limbed, with a square face covered with a dense stubble of whiskers, and deep-set grey eyes.

One of his favorite sports whenever I went to see him at his ranch in El Pino near Santa Rosa was shooting at a large rock in front of his house.

"*Vamos a ver,* got your gun with you?" he would say; then with his forty-five already drawn he would raise a puff of dust from the rock every time he squeezed the trigger. Occasionally I would hit the target and bring a sly grin to the old man's face.

"*Eso!* That's the way to shoot. A man should know how to handle a gun. Just in case; you never can tell."

On one of our trips together, we drove into the mountains

not far from Las Vegas looking for an old *trovador*[1] by the name of Apolinario Almanzares, whom we finally located in his flat-roofed adobe house at a village called Los Tres Ojitos. Almanzares was not his family name. No one knew what his original name might have been, for as a very young boy he had been bought from the Comanches by a man named Almanzares, who noticed that the jockey the Indians were using was white-skinned. He had probably been taken captive as a baby and had been brought up by the tribe.

We had no more than finished being introduced when a man appeared from behind the house with a pistol in one hand, and without a word of greeting burst out excitedly:

"I want you to witness the fact that my *primo* threatened my life, and if I kill him it will be in self-defense!"

Whoever the man was, he had learned somewhere that shooting in self-defense was not a crime, and he meant to "defend" himself from this *primo*,[2] provided he had witnesses to bear him out. My first impression was that the man had already disposed of his relative and was trying to establish a legal justification, but just then a second man appeared from the other side of the house also carrying a gun and telling us that he, too, was out to "defend" himself. Knowing something about the nature of these hotheaded mountaineers of San Miguel County, I was

[1] Until recently, local poets and versifiers wrote lyric and narrative poetry concerning everyday happenings in the villages of New Mexico. They also composed the tunes to which their ballads were sung, and many times sang their own compositions. These facile versifiers were very much in demand at parties and dances, where they were well paid for the verses they wrote in praise of a lady of someone's choice. *See,* Arthur L. Campa, *Spanish Folk Poetry in New Mexico.*

[2] Because of the fact that in the small towns of New Mexico the residents intermarried so much in the early days, most of them are related in one form or another. Oftentimes they simply express this relationship by calling each other "cousin." Strictly speaking a *primo* is a first cousin.

ready to leave the whole matter to the old-timers. Don Rafael was the first to speak, and he did so in a conversational tone:

"What are you fellows quarreling about? No need to shoot each other when you can settle your troubles right here with one of the best lawyers in the state."

When the eyes of the gun-toting *primos* were turned on me, the only stranger present, I started to explain that I was not a lawyer; but Don Rafael winked an eye at me surreptitiously, and that mischievous look admitted me to the bar in New Mexico.

Listening to their story, I found that one of the men had had the contract for driving the school wagon awarded to him because he had the largest number of children in his own family; but that the second one had now increased his family to an equal number of school children and therefore felt that the two should divide the contract and the proceeds between them. The dispute had led to threats and gun-toting, and finally ended in an appeal to Apolinario Almanzares, the old man of the mountain, who because of his years and experience was expected to arbitrate.

After the old troubadour got them to put up their guns, he asked Don Rafael to examine the case and draw up an agreement, which I was directed to write on my portable typewriter as the leading lawyer in Los Tres Ojitos. Between Don Rafael and me, we drew up as high-sounding a document as was ever written in San Miguel County, copied in part from the law book which Don Rafael always carried in his satchel, and left a number of impressive looking blanks for them to sign. "Whereas, there appeared before me . . . who is of sound mind . . . ." The "party of the first part" and the "party of the second part" were so intrigued with my portable *imprenta,* as they called the typewriter, that they forgot their quarrel and crowded around the "press machine" exclaiming in disbelief:

"*Qué diasque!* All it needs to do is talk!"

At the conclusion of the *convenio,* both men and all those present signed as participants or witnesses; they shook hands all around and swore that this was the way to settle disputes when there was a good lawyer handy. The thing that surprised them most, however, was our refusal to accept a fee. They offered to pay with live sheep instead of cash, adding an apology for not having any *dinero* on hand. As the fee seemed a little bulky, we declined it and drove away relieved and feeling like exemplary boy scouts. When we were out of ear-shot, Don Rafael remarked:

"How do you like being a lawyer?"

Don Rafael's knowledge of law was not profound, but his knowledge of human nature and particularly of the *gente,* his own people, was more useful to him than any book learning he might have had. His travels up and down the state had brought him into contact with all sorts of characters, including the Silva Gang,[3] Chávez y Chávez, Black Jack, and many others whose lives have been the subject of numerous publications. Through his association with badmen of the West, he had come into possession of a Sheffield blade that once had been the property of Billy the Kid. Don Rafael had acquired it in a very simple manner.

Chávez y Chávez, according to his story, had been paroled to him after conviction in order to attend to some personal matters on his farm before being locked up for life. Knowing that Chávez was treacherous and a fast draw, he put an empty gun into his holster where the outlaw could see it, but concealed a loaded one in a shoulder holster under his shirt. As it turned out, Chávez did not try to make a break, and in the two days

[3] The Silva Gang was a band of outlaws who operated around Las Vegas, New Mexico, at the end of the past century. This western outpost of the Santa Fe Trail harbored one of the worst gangs of rascals and cutthroats that ever infested the West. Such aliases as Doubleout Sam, Pegleg Dick, Hatchet-face Dick, Pawnee Bill, Dirty-face Mike, and Kickapoo George were among the long assortment of names that graced the rosters of notorious characters.

the men were together they became friendly. Before being re-turned to the penitentiary in Santa Fe, Chávez took a large knife, which he had hidden in a haystack, and gave it to Don Rafael, saying:

"You'd better have this; it may be useful to you on your ranch."

According to Don Rafael, Chávez had come into possession of this Bowie-like blade on a wager. He and Billy the Kid had bet their hunting knives at a horse race in Las Vegas several years before the Kid's fatal meeting with Pat Garrett; and the Kid's horse had come in last. The knife was a sturdy Sheffield blade, and the Kid always carried it with him. He never used it as a weapon; he was strictly a gunman. During one of our trips together, Don Rafael surprised me by taking the knife from his satchel and handing it to me.

"That's the Kid's knife. Keep it. You like things like that and I don't need it."

A cattleman who knew about the knife had been trying for some time to trade the old man out of it, but he always refused, saying that *un amigo* had left it with him. After the University of New Mexico Museum placed it on display, the cattleman came in to ask me how I had managed to get it. Don Rafael had his own way of doing things.

Whenever I went around to collect stories and traditional material I always took Don Rafael with me if he was available. He knew most of the old-timers and was better acquainted with the out-of-the-way places than anyone else in the region. There was hardly a spot of any importance that he could not spin a yarn about; a canyon, a peak, or a water hole would always remind him of something, and casually he would say:

"Do you see that peak over yonder? Every time I see it, it reminds me of what happened to my late *compadre . . .*"

Nothing more would be said until I asked: "Is that so? What

73

happened?" Don Rafael would reach for his *punche* bag, empty the right amount of tobacco on the palm of his thick hand, and grind it a bit with his thumb as he held the bag with his teeth. After carefully rolling his *cigarro* he would pass his tongue over the edge of the paper, light the tobacco with a kitchen match, draw the first puff, and settle back into the car seat to talk. He talked only when he was sure one was willing to listen, and in me he always had a receptive audience.

One day when we were driving east of Albuquerque on Highway 60, as we approached the little village of Encino over the eroded elevations, which eons ago had been mountains, Don Rafael pointed to a landmark on the Pedernal Mountains:

"Somewhere over that hill is supposed to be a diamond mine. They say that before the railroad came, the Indians used to trade diamonds to the *Comancheros,* and that the stones came from a deep cave in the Pedernal Mountains. One of the Romeros of Las Vegas is said to have traded a few yards of *bayeta* cloth for a handful of diamonds to an Indian on one of his trips to Visporte. [Westport, Kansas City]. That's how he got his start on the Santa Fe trade."

Don Rafael didn't know the exact location of the traditional diamond cave. All he knew was the story he told me as we drove past the Pedernal Mountains. With only this brief account to go on I knew I did not stand a chance of finding the cave, but I filed the story in the back of my mind for further reference. As it turned out, not very long after talking to the old man, I came across a person who not only knew the story but could also tell me the exact location of the cave. It all came about through a student in one of my classes, who, in the course of this association learned of my interest in local traditions. She was married to an engineer named Price employed by the New Mexico Highway Department. The story Mr. Price had heard made no mention of specific names but it spoke of a Santa Fe trader whose ox-wagon had strayed away from the rest of the train during a heavy blizzard in the Pedernal Mountains not far from the village of Encino.

While wandering lost in the storm, the driver came upon the sheltered side of a mountain and drove his oxen as close as he could get them against a projection on the west side of a cliff. This windbreak provided shelter for him and his team until the storm subsided and he could get back to his outfit. He got off the wagon, and as he stepped to the ground he noticed an opening on the side of the mountain, which to a man trying to weather a snowstorm was a welcome sight. He walked into a cave, sensing the warm air from within, but discovered that he could not go beyond a few steps because there was a sudden drop about thirty feet deep. He went back to the entrance and amused himself by tossing pebbles and small stones into the far recesses of the cave. After a while he noticed that some of the stones he was gathering were a sort of crystalline quartz. He sorted out a few of the best ones to take back to his children in Las Vegas.

Eventually the storm blew itself out and the trader left the mountain windbreak to go in search of the rest of the train. By sundown he rejoined it, and continued on the way to Kansas City. He never gave much thought to the pebbles he had picked up in the cave until one morning when one fell out of his pocket as he stood talking to the train boss. Attracted by its glitter, the boss asked what it was and the driver told him.

"I've got a handful of them in my pocket. Found them in that cave where I holed up during the storm. Thought my kids would like 'em to play with."

After examining the little stones more closely, the boss suggested that they might be valuable.

"They look awful pretty. If I were you I'd have a jeweler look at 'em in Kansas City."

The driver followed the *mayordomo's* advice and took the crystals to a jeweler shortly after the train arrived. To his surprise he was told that the playthings he had picked up so casually were genuine diamonds. Immediately he asked to have one of them set in a ring for his wife, but was informed by the jeweler that they would have to be cut and polished either in New York or Europe before he could set any of them.

This story is not very different from the one I had heard Don Rafael tell, but it had the added incentive of the location of the cave. Mr. Price and I arranged to make the trip to the Pedernal Mountains as soon as the spring thaw had run off, when it was dry enough to drive through the brush. Mrs. Price prepared the lunch and took her 150-pound St. Bernard dog to keep her company while her husband and I would let ourselves down a rope into a cave in the days when speleology was not a popular science. We drove across the salt flats west of the Pecos, and just before reaching Encino left Highway 60 and followed a trail north through the scrub and juniper until we came to an overhanging escarpment, under which was the opening to a natural cave. The mouth was big enough for us to stand in with room to spare, but a few steps farther on there was a thirty-foot drop. We tied a stout rope to a tree near the entrance and let ourselves down to the next level. The first thing we did was to search the floor for anything that might look like a crystal, but all we could find was smooth-worn pebbles.

We explored this subterranean chamber for a distance of about twenty yards and came to a place where the floor was cut by a fissure, which increased in depth and width until we found ourselves walking on two opposite ledges. The widening crevasse eventually absorbed the floor of the cave and left us no walking surface, and so we retraced our steps hoping to enter another opening branching out from the main chamber. Halfway back we dangled our ropes into the fissure and found them too short to attempt a second descent to a lower level. Mr. Price stopped for a moment to gather a few specimens from the wall while I continued on my way back, thinking that he was keeping up with me on the opposite side. Suddenly I heard a call, and simultaneously there was a dull, loud thud followed by a cloud of dust through which the beam of my torch was unable to penetrate. Much to my relief, I was able to make out a moment later the moving form of a man running toward me on the ledge where I was standing. It was Price. His side of the cave had given way and he had leaped forward with it, landing on the opposite side as the dry bank cascaded into the bottom of the crevasse.

Another bust of speed through the choking dust brought us safely to solid ground. The sound of a second cave-in far in the interior told us that we should not be able to explore the dislodged banks of the cave for a good while. For the time being we thought it best to return to the surface. Going back on the rope was not as easy as the descent, but there was the incentive of a good lunch awaiting us; and so we pulled our way back in Alpine fashion until we reached daylight and clean, fresh air to breathe.

After a cool drink of water, Price looked at me through dust-covered eyelashes and remarked:

"That was damned close!"

Apparently the diamonds were not for us. There is a strong belief among the Spanish-speaking population of the Southwest that buried treasures are destined for a particular person, and that anyone not favorably predetermined by fate will never succeed in keeping a treasure even though he should find it. Nicolaza López de Valenzuela knew this, but her faith in the existence of the treasure she had heard so much about since childhood led her to defy the Spanish tradition when she began digging in the middle of the kitchen floor of the ranch house she had inherited from her mother, Doña Martina de la O López.

The farm was known as a *ranchito,* a nine-acre plot of land almost hidden by the Río Grande near the village of Ysleta, Texas. At one end of the property, toward the river where the land rose to a flat shelf, there was an L-shaped adobe house, built about 1790 by a band of men whose main occupation was intercepting the *conductas* on the Camino Real. Back of the house was a thick forest of cottonwoods and willows by the edge of the river, and the front side was conveniently hidden by a heavy tangle of *garambullo,* which had grown up undisturbed for no one knew how long. This thick and thorny bush is a greyish-green shrub usually covered in the early spring with red berries twice the size of an ordinary pea. It makes a favorite hiding place for cottontail rabbits and a convenient cover for rattlesnakes during the hot summer months.

El ranchito de la Ysleta, as the family came to call their small farm, had been bought by the head of the family shortly after the Civil War, not because he was anxious to own the property, but because it was a condition laid down by his future bride before she would agree to marry him. Don Juan López, a member of a well-known family in Chihuahua, had been struck with wanderlust when he was a young boy and had gone to live with a Santa Fe trader in Kansas City, where he had remained until he attained his majority. Like many young men in search of adventure in the West at that time, he joined the Santa Fe trade and in a few years became *mayordomo* of one of the outfits operated by Tolland and Ochoa.

On one of his trips to New Mexico in the early sixties, Don Juan met Doña Martina, the belle of the village of Doña Ana, and reputedly the best polka dancer in the Mesilla Valley. She was a first generation descendant of the De la O family, which in 1829 had been granted by the Mexican government a strip of land twenty-two miles along the river from Doña Ana south to Tortugas below the present city of Las Cruces. Don Juan left the Santa Fe trade for awhile to remain in the Mesilla Valley as a United States marshal, and also to pursue his interest in the young girl; but she would not agree to wed him until he settled down with a house and some property to his name.

Juan López, like many pioneers of that day, was strong-willed and reluctant to give up the freedom he had grown up with, but Martina's charms outweighed his objections and eventually led him to buy a piece of property by the Río Grande, about sixty miles southeast of Doña Ana. The place was supposed to have been at one time an outlaw hideout. Not long after the young couple moved into the *ranchito,* bringing a yoke of oxen and a fine saddle horse, they began to hear rumors among the scattered residents of Ysleta that the highwaymen who had once lived on the property had cached their loot somewhere within the house they were now living in. They listened politely to these stories but were too busy getting settled to embark upon a treasure hunt when there were more important things to do. Land was the only treasure that appealed to the young bride, and she lost no time in locating another good section to homestead a few miles north of their little farm by some foothills known as the Loma Tewa. Once again Don Juan was talked into acquiring additional property, to which he no longer objected now that his family was beginning to increase. By the time their second child was born, they had built there a large adobe ranch house with three-foot walls, a *zaguán,* a patio, and a corral to protect their stock from the forays of the Apache chief, Victorio, who was then on the warpath.

The Ysleta farm took a secondary role and was soon turned over to a man named Martín Apodaca, who worked the land in traditional *al partido* fashion, that is, on a share basis. This

79

left Don Juan free to devote all his energies to the newly acquired property, where among other things he started a good
herd of cattle and planted an orchard with seedlings brought
from his former home in Kansas City. Once a year he went to
the *ranchito* to collect his share from the sale of the annual crop.
Things went along smoothly for several years, but Martín gradually took to the bottle and had difficulty accounting for his
patrón's share. Finally, in 1890 the share-cropper dissipated his
own share and the portion due to Don Juan. When the latter
rode by one Sunday afternoon early in the fall to collect his rent,
Martín Apodaca was in no condition to render accounts. The
spirits of *aguardiente* had completely changed the usually quiet
man into an irritable and belligerent individual, so much so that
when Don Juan mentioned the share he had come to collect,
he answered defiantly:

"I don't owe you anything. Get out or I'll shoot you!"

Don Juan was already walking toward his horse when he
heard this threat and therefore he didn't see Apodaca reach behind the door for his shotgun. He turned around, and as he did
so he uttered his last words: "Shoot, you drunken fool!"

Martín did just that, and the proud husband of Doña Martina fell mortally wounded with the reins of his horse still in
his hand.

Weeds grew the following year on the *ranchito,* field mice
made their nests in the house, and the old pear tree in the front
yard housed the family of a mockingbird, whose song was the
only sound heard on the now abandoned farm by the Río Grande.
No one was willing to tread too soon upon soil where the well-
known rancher had been killed. The memory of the *aguardiente-*
crazed *mediero* lingered about the place and added more fuel
to the stories about the *entierro* left by the outlaws.

Once again, as in the days when the young couple first settled on the land, people began to see flames shooting upward on

rainy days. The house was "on fire" many times according to the neighbors, but it was never consumed. One dark night, a woman named Dionisia who lived in a *jacal* not far from the entrance to the farm, saw a lighted candle going round and round in the front yard. Speculation about the treasure was more than a passing fancy among some members of the López family, particularly to one of the more impressionable daughters, Nicolaza, known affectionately as "Nico." She thought about the outlaws' hoard in that lonely *ranchito* many evenings before going to sleep by the Loma Tewa, but her insistence that they try to look for it was met by her practical-minded mother with stern refusals.

Doña Martina, now a widow, was too busy trying to run her affairs to think about such things, and in the back of her religious mind she thought it was improper to go looking for treasures "where rust doth corrupt." The only treasure on the little farm that interested her was the corn her *peones* planted every spring and harvested in the fall. She solved the problem of having to give the Ysleta land *al partido,* by sending men to tend the crop. She still remembered the unhappy experience of the share-basis agreement with Martín Apodaca, and the tragic memory strengthened her resolve never to try it again. Every month during the growing season she would drive by in her buckboard to look at the progress of the corn crop. As she stopped to open the barbed-wire gate at the entrance, Dionisia, the neighbor by the fence, would hail her and offer her the usual cup of hot coffee of western hospitality.

On one of her visits to Ysleta, Doña Martina stopped to share the customary coffee with Dionisia and was chided by the old neighbor for not having stopped on her last visit.

"Doña Martina, why didn't you stop for a cup of coffee the last time you came by? I knew you came late because I saw the light at the house, but it doesn't make any difference how late it is. Just drive right up and sit down with Nicolás and me even if it is only for a minute. Why, the last time I fell asleep in a chair expecting you to stop on the way back!"

Doña Martina was puzzled by this talk, and explained to her hospitable neighbor that she hadn't been at the farm at all. Not wishing to appear unappreciative of her neighbor's well-meaning concern, she said no more, but it made her wonder if anyone had been around the farm in her absence. On the way to the house she watched the lane carefully for tracks that would indicate a visitor, and even expected to find the padlock broken open at the door of the ranch house. There was no sign of anyone's presence; things were exactly as she had left them. "Poor Dionisia," she thought; "she's still thinking about that old treasure."

The young daughter, Nicolaza, grew up and married an El Paso businessman named Valenzuela. He knew nothing about farming and cared less for it, but when his wife told him about the treasure in Ysleta he decided it was time he took up farming. He and his wife talked it over with Doña Martina who, glad to rid herself of the bothersome *ranchito,* turned it over to her daughter as part of her eventual inheritance. Valenzuela made it known that the old house needed remodeling, and so began to spend every weekend on the farm taking down the walls, one adobe at a time. His painstaking efforts yielded nothing more than an aching back over the weekend, but there still remained other places to explore before the indefatigable businessman would give up. Some prankster in the family, who guessed what Valenzuela was searching for, buried an old earthen pot where he would run into it, and placed a dime in it, with a note reading: "Behold the treasure of Ysleta!"

For a few months after the little joke, the treasure-hunter was not seen around the farm and for a very good reason; he had taken ill with a dangerous nose infection and had died within a matter of weeks. A second man associated with the farm was now dead and a second-generation woman had been widowed. Nico's ardor cooled considerably after her husband's death. She turned the property back to her mother and went to live in California with one of her daughters.

A couple of years later, while bathing in Long Beach one day, she was attracted by a crowd of people waiting in line to go inside a tent where a very unusual fortuneteller was plying his trade, and performing the most amazing feats of divination. She was urged by her friends to go in and have her fortune told. To her great surprise, as she set foot in the tent, an ominous-sounding voice greeted her by name and anticipated the answer to what she had in mind to ask:

"You have come to see me about a treasure located in a farmhouse in Ysleta, Texas. The answer is yes, the treasure does exist. But you are not the one to recover it."

Stunned by this unexpected dictum, Nicolaza left California and returned to her home in El Paso. She tried to forget the treasure but the fortuneteller's words preyed on her mind so strongly that she decided to talk the matter over with one of her daughters. Young Elsie had a lot of spirit; she was the sort of person who would enjoy looking for a treasure, particularly if it meant circumventing a soothsayer's prophecy.

Mother and daughter waited patiently until they could find a man whom they could trust, for they thought that by having a third party do the digging they might break the soothsayer's prediction. In the village of Ysleta they finally found an honest, simple man well suited for their plan, and began to sound him out, asking him if he had ever heard about the treasure in the old ranch house. He knew about it, but more important yet was his willingness to dig for it on a share basis. They sat down with this man, whom we shall call Pedro, and worked out the plan they were to follow, being careful not to reveal to him what the fortuneteller had said, although they did mention that the treas-

83

ure was definitely supposed to exist. They were to go to the house after all the neighborhood was asleep and dig in the middle of the kitchen floor, the only place Nico's husband had not searched.

On the appointed day, the two women drove down from El Paso, picked up Pedro, and made their way quietly into the house remodeled by Valenzuela. The man drew a five-foot square in the center of the earthen floor while the women covered the windows with some black cloth they had brought along for the purpose. By the light of an oil lantern the operation began in earnest. The centuries-old earthen floor was broken with a heavy crowbar and a pick, but once the first foot of hardened mud was dislodged, Pedro used his shovel freely. The women looked at each other from time to time in ecstatic anticipation, but with an apparent uncertainty every time they remembered what they knew by tradition and through the fortuneteller's prophecy. They took turns at holding the lantern for Pedro, who by midnight had disappeared into the hole he was digging. The loose earth had completely filled the room, and mother and daughter sat precariously on the piles trying to light the man's crowded working space below.

Pedro, tired of digging, was getting ready to declare that the treasure was nothing more than an old wives' tale when his shovel rang loudly as he plunged it indifferently into the middle of the excavation. The sound electrified all three and at the same time sent a cold chill through them. The two women looked at each other with clenched teeth, almost terrified now that the moment had arrived. Down in the hole, Pedro was scraping the bottom carefully and, as he leaned over to examine the chest, of which the outline was now clearly revealed, he went limp and collapsed.

Nico and Elsie screamed and held tight to each other when they saw Pedro's knees buckle under him. It was two o'clock

84

in the morning; they were alone in an abandoned farmhouse with a man who had suddenly collapsed and was probably dead. If they called in someone to help, the secret would be out. There was only one thing to do. They dragged Pedro out as best they could and tried to revive him, but the inert body did not respond. On the very threshold of success they had a dying man on their hands. This was an irony of fate, something they had not counted on.

They dragged the unconscious man into their car and took him down to a relative in the village, who called a doctor after he learned what had happened. When Pedro came to, the three agreed to do nothing more that morning, but to return to the farmhouse at noon the same day and finish the job. The mother and daughter stayed in Ysleta the rest of the morning, too restless and nervous to return to El Paso. At the hour agreed, the three drove down to the digging in anticipation of wealth and fortune, and elated at having gainsaid the old fortuneteller.

When they reached the door ready to put the key in the padlock, they were stunned to find it wide open. They rushed in, climbed over the mound of earth in the kitchen, and peered down into the bottom of a deep hole, where a rectangular imprint of a chest told them that someone had been there ahead of them. Nicolaza Valenzuela stood speechless, the ominous words uttered by the soothsayer back in California ringing in her ears:

"The treasure does exist, but you are not the one to recover it."

CHAPTER 7

TREASURES HID IN THE FIELDS

◆

EDUARDO MEDINA wanted to be a schoolteacher, and he fulfilled his wish when he graduated from the University of New Mexico before Hitler had become a threat in Europeon affairs. Eduardo was born and reared in one of the northern counties of New Mexico, Rio Arriba, the scene of countless family feuds and a hotbed of New Mexican politics. The votes from Rio Arriba County can swing a closely contested election today, and sometimes even bring about a Congressional investigation.

Young Eduardo had been nurtured from childhood in the traditional lore abounding in this isolated countryside, and had heard stories about buried treasures from the time he was old enough to sit by the fireplace on his grandfather's knee and crack piñon nuts during long winter evenings. From older members of his family, from friends who dropped in to visit on Sundays, and from some of the Indians who worked on his father's farm, he had acquired a head full of "lost mines" and "Indian treasures." These stories, told leisurely and convincingly by narrators who enjoyed telling them as much as the young boy enjoyed listening to them, filled him with a desire to go out and search for hidden wealth.

As Eduardo grew older, he became more discerning and practical. The indefinite settings of these stories, such as "in a canyon not far from here" or "back in the days of the Indian uprisings," were too vague for him to start on a search. He wanted to lay his hands on a real treasure map. He wanted to have someone tell him that on some definite spot a certain person had buried a specified number of gold coins, bullion, or jewels. But such an opportunity never came about in the little village in Rio Arriba County.

While Eduardo was still a young boy, his family went to live in Alcalde along the east bank of the upper Río Grande on the road to Taos. Here he made the acquaintance of an interesting old sheepherder by the name of Nicolás. Like most *borregueros* in New Mexico, Nicolás had never married and lived alone, tending his sheep over the green ranges of the Sangre de Cristo Mountains or down in the lowlands where the grass grew tall. He had worked over thirty years for one of the large sheep owners in the northern part of the state, and although he was paid in cash regularly he was never known to put a cent of it in any of the nearby banks, nor had he placed it in anyone's trust.

As Eduardo grew older he began to wonder what his old friend, the sheepherder, did with his money. It was obvious that he never spent any of it. His wants were few and the *patrón* furnished him with groceries and an occasional bottle of "Taos lightning" along with the cast-off clothing he always wore. One day while hunting in the mountains during the deer season, Eduardo came across his friend, the sheepherder, sitting on a ledge watching his flock graze on the mountainside. The young man sat down to rest awhile and chat with the old man. In the course of their conversation they touched upon money matters. Eduardo had enough of the sheepherder's confidence to venture a personal question regarding finances.

"Nicolás," he said, "why don't you put away your money in a bank so you'll have it some day when you are too old to work any longer?"

87

"No, *hijo*. My son, I don't trust any of these smooth-handed crooks. *Manos lisas!* That's what they are."

Anyone with smooth hands, without the calluses of hard work, was not an honest man to Nicolás. *"Manos lisas!"* was his way of summing up the contempt he felt for city people. Eduardo knowing it was useless to press the subject he had so cautiously broached, changed to something else. He still had to learn what the old man did with his earnings.

Nicolás was a hardy specimen accustomed to outdoor life—preferred it to living indoors and was never known to be sick. The people in Alcalde used to say he was too mean to die: *"Cosa mala nunca muere."* They also joked with him about his age by telling him that he was going to remain for seed: *"Te quedarás para semilla."* Nicolás took this friendly bantering good-naturedly and went along chuckling to himself.

In the same village of Alcalde there lived one of the very

small number of Anglo-Americans in that part of the country, a man named Clark, whose grocery store was one of the few places frequented by Nicolás whenever he happened to be in the village. He would sit around the store for awhile; then, after eating a lunch of canned sardines, store bread, and a raw onion, he would saunter down to an apple orchard by the river and take a siesta. Before leaving, he would go back to the store, pick up the groceries provided by his *patrón* and climb up the narrow path to a one-room adobe house he owned on a hill at the far end of town.

On one of his infrequent visits to Alcalde, Nicolás arrived late at night, and left his nondescript sheep dogs by the door where they usually slept. When the villagers noticed them the following morning, they supposed he would be down to the *Americano's* store later in the day; but to their surprise, Nicolás was not seen there that day nor the next. A party of woodcutters coming down the mountain path by the door of the hut were attracted by the incessant howling of the dogs, and believing that the howling of dogs at night presages tragedy or *mal agüero*, they spread the alarm in the village. Eduardo was one of the first to arrive at the sheepherder's shack, where Nicolás was found lying on his cot just as he had come in from the mountains, his shoes still on and his hands over his chest.

The death of Nicolás was a shock to the villagers. People had come to think of him as indestructible. It was hard to believe that the little adobe on the edge of town would no longer be a landmark referred to as *"La casita de Nicolás."* The old man had no living relatives so far as was known; thus Eduardo was selected by reason of his close friendship with the deceased, to make the necessary arrangements for his burial.

After Nicolás had been laid away in the village cemetery, Eduardo and two of his friends assigned by him to look after the property, took inventory of his meager belongings. There was nothing of value in the house, but in going through his rawhide knapsack one of the men found a small wooden box wrapped in a piece of sheepskin. As he took the box in his hands, Eduardo remembered the conversation he had had with Nicolás on the mountainside during the deer-hunting season. So here was the secret of the old man's reluctance to bank his earnings! Here was a real treasure. Eduardo felt a little disappointed at the simple way in which it had been discovered. He would have preferred something a little more complicated with mysterious markings and treasure maps. The box was locked, and as no key was found after searching everywhere, the lid was pried open.

Instead of the bank notes they had expected to find inside, the box contained only a heavy piece of neatly folded paper. Disappointment gave way to speculation when Eduardo unfolded it. It was a simple chart marking the location of a large pine tree on the edge of the forest. There was also some poorly scribbled directions telling the finder to dig three feet below the surface at the foot of the tree on the side nearest the house and toward the setting sun. A large rock with the initial N was to be found at the specified depth, and three feet farther down he would find another wooden box. A last sentence was written at the bottom of the chart thanking anyone good enough to give him a Christian burial. Nicolás had had faith in the goodness of his fellow men.

The three men decided not to mention their find to the residents of the village. After Nicolás was forgotten, or was at least out of the minds of the people, they planned to gather at the house and locate the tree where the treasure was buried. They felt certain that the old sheepherder had devised this means to protect his money. Eduardo was sorry to have lost his old friend, but with a sense of realism, was glad that he had provided him with the very thing he had always wanted, a treasure hunt. It was not the actual money that intrigued Eduardo, it was the idea of searching for a hidden treasure, a real *entierro* at last!

A few weeks passed, and the day was set for the three men to go in search of the tree mentioned by Nicolás. They had no trouble finding it; the old man's directions were brief but clear. Eduardo's excitement increased with every shovelful of earth they dug. In a short while they came to a large rock, which was removed for closer inspection, and a well-defined *N* was found chiseled on its flat side. Three more feet of earth were shoveled out by the men taking turns, until they reached what they had come to find: a wooden box wrapped in sheepskin like the first one.

Eduardo realized now his lifelong ambition; he had found a treasure map, had followed the instructions given therein, and had located the chest, the contents of which he was about to view at this very moment. The two other men, no less excited, could tell by its weight that the box was filled with paper money —it had to be bank notes because nothing rattled when they shook it. They pried open the lid and to their surprise found a large roll of receipts signed by Mr. Clark, the store owner. At the bottom of the box, under the sheaf of receipts, was a properly executed deed turning over some property to a girl named Andrea Trujillo.

The apple orchard where Nicolás used to take his siesta on summer afternoons had been paid for by monthly installments over many years, and through the legal documents at the bottom of the little wooden box, his "natural" daughter, as the document declared, unaware that the old sheepherder on the hillside was her father, came into possession of an apple orchard in Alcalde. Eduardo had found a treasure, for the orchard was a valuable piece of property, but again the old Spanish tradition was upheld. A finder does not keep the treasure unless so decreed by Fate, and she had never arranged for Eduardo to be the son of Nicolás!

But Fate was not so cruel in the case of Tía Anastacia's family. The first time I saw the old matriarch she was sitting in the shade of a large cottonwood tree in front of her neatly-plastered house with a sewing basket at her feet and something in her lap that looked very much like a blouse. As I watched the hundred-and-fifteen year-old woman ply her needle with nimble fingers, I wondered if she was working simply by touch or was actually able to see what she was doing.

"Tía Anastacia," I asked, "aren't you straining your eyes sewing without your glasses?"

When she looked up to answer me I noticed that her eyes were clear.

"No, son, the Lord has given me good eyes to see with."

Tía Anastacia was one of the few Senecú Indians left from the original village below the Río Grande near El Paso, and like many of her people she had become completely Hispanized to the point where she no longer spoke her own dialect. She had a daughter named Mariana to whom the neighbors usually referred as *"La India Mariana"* alluding to her racial origin, although this appellation was never used in direct address. Mariana was married to a man named Nacianceno Pedregón, a short, stocky, hard-working farmer reputedly deaf, or conveniently so. He was aware of the infirmity attributed to him and never missed an opportunity to make light of it. Once when I called to him: *"Oiga!,"* meaning "Hear me," he answered:

"I do hear, and when they say *'Tenga* [have some],' I can hear a lot better."

When the family of Tía Anastacia moved to the El Paso Valley about 1870, they did not own a comfortable house nor did they have any horses. They settled in a gypsy-like cave dug

into the sandhills of what once had been the north bank of the
Río Grande. These perpendicular *lomas* were used to shelter
many of the early pioneer residents who came to the valley below El Paso after the Civil War, and the family of Tía Anastacia
was one of the poorest of these settlers. Very soon after coming
to live in their dugout, the whole family went to work putting
up a sort of front-room addition, a *jacal* made with a framework
of cottonwood limbs filled with tight bunches of *cachanilla,* a
slender dry-land reed with soft and abundant leaves on upward-
growing straight stems; and plastered it inside and out with
adobe mud. From the *bosque*[1] by the Río Grande they brought
loads of *jara* reeds for the corrals of their nimble-footed Mexican
goats, the milk and cheese of which provided some of the family
income as well as part of the food.

The men went to work clearing land for the large landholders in the valley, and the womenfolk carded wool, washed
clothes, and did the *molienda* (corn-grinding) for bread and
tortillas in the days when flour mills were few and far between.
The young boys had their chores, too. As soon as the goats were
milked, they took them to the *lomas* behind the *jacal* to feed on
the grama-covered mesas where mesquite pods were sweet and
tender in the early summer. During the hot season, the goats
rested in the shade of arroyo banks or under some century-old
mesquite, while the boys played *pitarilla,*[2] the traditional game
of the Mexican sheepherder.

[1] Before the drainage canals were put in the valley below El Paso, the
land alongside the river was covered with a thick growth of reeds and cottonwood trees. It was customary for the ranchers along the border to get their
trees for sheds and barns as well as for planting from these thick woods referred
to as *bosques.* These "forests" were a good hideout for questionable characters
of all sorts.

[2] *Pitarrilla* is sometimes referred to as "New Mexican checkers," although
it hardly resembles this game. The board consists of a rectangle with four lines,
two centered on the sides, and two from corner to corner, all lines crossing at

Once in a while the boys would drive their goats near another flock belonging to an old patriarch, whose flowing white beard and walking staff gave him the appearance of a Biblical prophet. Don Damasio was a kindly old man, tall, thin, and blue-eyed; he was part Irish, with a sharp tongue for those who crossed him, and an entertaining stock of stories for children, whom he loved much more than his goats. As soon as Tía Anastacia's grandchildren located the old man by listening to the *cencerro* of the *macho cabrío,* the lead goat's bell, they would descend on Don Damasio begging for a story. At first he would feign great displeasure, threatening to tell their grandmother if they didn't get back to their goats; but when his conscience had been assuaged by these threats, he would sit down in the shade, place both hands upon his staff for support, and begin moving his chin whiskers like his cud-chewing goats lying under the mesquites all around them.

Aside from the stock of *cuentos* which Don Damasio used to preface with the usual: *"Est-era un rey que tenía tres hijas,"* ("Once there was a king who had three daughters,"), there was a local legend about a treasure that the boys always enjoyed despite their having heard it many times. It was the story of a Spaniard named Miranda who buried some gold he was carrying when the Comanches attacked his pack train.

Don Trinidad Miranda was returning from Santa Fe with a party of traders when they were surprised by a band of Comanches, and before they could safely reach the crossing at El Paso the Indians cut them off and forced them to the north bank of the Río Grande. There the men scattered, some swimming across, leaving their pack animals behind. Don Trinidad kept under cover of the trees in the *bosque* along the river hoping

---

the center of the board. The idea is to move three counters consisting of little matchsticks if played on the sand, until they are lined up in any direction. *See, The Spanish-American Song and Dance Book,* 67.

to avoid discovery and save the gold he was carrying in his
saddlebags. But the mule he was riding balked at the water's
edge, and with the Comanches close behind him he decided to
put the gold in a cooking pot and bury it on the riverbank close
to a tree. The Comanches were so close that he had no time to
carve a marker on the tree; in his hurry he thought he could
recognize the place again. Before he could dive into the river
he was cut off by the Comanche scouts and taken prisoner. His
feet were securely tied.

95

That same night while the rest of the Indian camp slept in a clump of trees by the river, Don Trinidad worked his way quietly to the bank, rolled gently into the water, and was carried downstream by the current, unnoticed by his captors. As he reached the opposite bank he thought he saw some Comanches moving among the trees where a few minutes before he had been planning his escape. Once out of the water, he untied his feet and began walking toward the Spanish settlements that lay south of the river. The following day after walking over the dry plains of Chihuahua, he saw the dust of a moving caravan along the Camino Real and hurried to intercept it, but kept at a distance for fear it might turn out to be an Apache party on some raiding expedition. At nightfall he approached the camp-fires cautiously and discovered that it was a *conducta* on its way to the fair at Chihuahua. Although he was exhausted and thirsty he quickened his pace and almost ran into the guard posted around the camp.

He told the *mayordomo* and the muleteers about the Coman-che attack and his escape the previous night. It was not a new story to them in those days of hostile Indians roving the plains and raiding the pack trains along the trails of the Southwest.

"What were you carrying?" asked the *mayordomo*.

Don Trinidad mentioned the usual inventory of goods, camping equipment, and other impedimenta, but said nothing of the cooking pot he had buried along the banks of the Río Grande. That, he thought, could keep until he went back to dig it up.

The following spring, Trinidad Miranda went back to the Río Grande not far from where the present city of El Paso is now situated, and tried to locate the cottonwood grove where he had been surprised by the Comanches, but high water had erased from the landscape the picture he had kept in his mind all those months. Even the channel of the river had moved away, leaving no clue that might lead the disappointed trader to the gold, which now lay buried in the mud and muck of the swollen stream.

At the end of his narrative, Don Damasio would pat the little boys on the head and say to them: "Now run along, back to your goats and keep an eye for that pot of gold. Maybe you'll run across it. Who knows?"

The family of Tía Anastacia worked diligently for many years and eventually saved enough to buy a couple of acres of land along the river bottom not far from their *jacal* on the hillside. They managed a good crop of beans and corn when the river was high, but there were years when the drought made life difficult for them. The large landholders along the valley began installing gasoline water pumps to tide them over during the dry periods, but to a man like Pedregón this was a luxury he never hoped for.

Several years went by with the monotonous rhythm of this sunny land; Nacianceno grew older, the children grew up, and Tía Anastacia accumulated years without much change in her wrinkled face. Early in the spring of 1905 the father and one of his boys were plowing the last furrow with their plodding oxen when the boy remarked, "Look, Papa, you broke some pottery with your plow back there."

He stopped the all-too-willing oxen, walked back a few steps, and kicked with his toe a few of the pieces on the freshly turned ground. As he stooped over to pick up one of the fragments, he noticed a yellow disc partly buried in the ground, and dug around it with his gnarled fingers. He held it up, rubbed it on his pants leg, and looked at it again incredulously. "Give me the *garrocha*," he said excitedly to his son.

The son handed him the prodding stick and with it he began

97

digging around the place where the coin had showed up. The plow had sheared the top off a clay pot and had uncovered what to the old man seemed a fortune. The son was sent for the mother, and Nacianceno stood fast by the uncovered pot for fear that the treasure might vanish from his sight. Mariana came running to the field, and together with her husband transferred the contents of the pot into her apron.

That day they plowed no more. Back in their *jacalito,* the little hut that was their home, they counted over and over each piece at a time, surrounded by their children and the old grandmother Anastacia. They kept cautioning the children to say nothing of their find to anyone, but even if the children had said nothing, the neighbors guessed that something had happened in Tía Anastacia's household. The old *jacalito* was torn down and replaced with a spacious adobe house. By the time summer came around, there was a sturdy corral back of the house with two young roans instead of the overworked oxen. The one item that could not be explained by mere economies and years of industrious labor was a six-inch gasoline pump, which the dealer came all the way from El Paso to install.

Eventually even the neighbors got used to the good life of the old woman's household so that when she died at the unbelievable age of one hundred thirty-five years, everyone had forgotten that they had ever lived in a lean-to on the hillside of what once had been the north bank of the Río Grande. The daughter Mariana followed her mother a few years later, although only a middle-aged woman by her mother's standards of longevity, and her husband Nacianceno soon joined them. Four generations have lived on the same land and in the same adobe house, now equipped with conveniences unheard-of in the Indian days of Tía Anastacia. No one speaks of the family treasure plowed up on that early spring day years ago by a hard-working grandfather, but the descendants of the venerated Tía smile and shrug their shoulders when asked about it.

Was this the pot of gold concealed by Don Trinidad Miranda during the Comanche attack? Is this the story that Don Damasio, the old patriarch of the mesquite-covered hills used to tell the little goatherds in the arroyo banks near El Paso? *Quién sabe!*

CHAPTER 8

THE JESUIT TREASURE OF BAMOA

◆

THE EXPULSION of the Jesuits from Mexico in the eighteenth century has given rise to a number of legends that speak of gold, silver coins, and church treasures left concealed by the churchmen when they made their forced exodus from the mission fields of Arizona and Mexico. Many treasure hunters have searched for this fabulous wealth over the past two centuries, but the few coins and occasional relics unearthed by hopeful seekers do not measure up to the glowing accounts of "muleloads of coined silver reales" of which tradition speaks in the American Southwest. Despite the meager success in finding anything of consequence, the stories about Jesuit *entierros* persists, particularly in those places where their missions were established.

Among the many treasures known to tradition, there is one associated with the little village of Bamoa along the south bank of the Sinaloa River in western Mexico which, through the circumstance of history, has been linked with the American Southwest since the day it was founded. This relatively unimportant settlement lies a few miles north of Compostela, the place from which Francisco Vásquez de Coronado set out on his expedition in 1540 to explore the land of the Gran Quivira. Bamoa is also the place where Cabeza de Vaca ended the arduous odyssey begun in Florida in 1528, the place where after eight years' wandering, led by friendly Indians, he ran into the slave-hunting expedition of a captain named Diego de Alcaraz.

At first the men could not believe that the weather-worn De Vaca was a Spaniard, but when he fell on his knees and made the sign of the cross they brought him before Captain Alcaraz,[1] to whom the ragged soldier identified himself in poorly remembered Castilian. The Captain suggested that the Indian guides be added to his slave collection, but the grateful De Vaca insisted that they be rewarded for their services in guiding him to the Spanish settlements, by giving them land upon which to settle. They selected a location on the banks of the Sinaloa River and named the place Bamoa, "Flower by the Water." This event established the first link in the chain of events that in the succeeding centuries connected the Southwest with the tropical village of Bamoa.

The village never grew to any considerable extent in the years that followed its founding and even today it may not be as large as it was in the sixteenth century; but the Jesuits made it an important center of their Nío Mission when they extended their work into northern Sinaloa. Three principal buildings were erected during the seventeenth century: the church, part of which is still standing; a *Colegio,* which eventually became a sort of vocational school; and the *Casa del Misionero.* After the village was abandoned by the Jesuits, the school became a stopping place on the overland mail route for the *diligencia* or stage,

[1] In 1645, Father Andrés Perez de Ribas published his *Triunfos de Nuestra Santa Fe* in Madrid. In 1944 his works were re-edited by "Layac" in Mexico City, and published in three volumes. *See,* I, 148–49 for the account of Captain Alcaraz, who mistook the returning De Vaca and his three companions for Indians one hundred leagues north of Compostela. The village of Bamoa, according to Ribas, was established about four leagues down the Sinaloa River from the place where the encounter was made.

and as a result the schoolhouse came to be known as *La Casa de la Posta*.[2] This is the name by which it is known to treasure-hunters today.

No one knows exactly how many Indians settled in Bamoa in 1536, and not until 1784 were there any census figures available. By then, according to the records in the Mexican archives, there were 342 Indians and 42 Spaniards in Bamoa, while in the nearby city of Sinaloa just across the river there were 2,240 Spaniards and 166 Indians. Among the Spaniards living in Bamoa were Jesuit missionaries whose main interest was the conversion of the Indians, while Sinaloa was a strictly Spanish settlement with a few Indian servants.

According to tradition, the Jesuits used many of their students of the vocational school to exploit the rich mineral resources of the region, and the gold panned from the placers of the Sierra watershed found its way into the candelabra and other religious ornaments that adorned their churches. The commercial activities of the order are not unknown to history and since Sinaloa has a wealth of mineral resources, it is not unlikely that the good padres conducted a search for precious metals. Until recently it was customary for the villagers throughout the state of Sinaloa to sell *oro bruto* (gold nuggets) to merchants and to travelers coming through on the Sud Pacífico Railroad. The country also abounds in semi-precious stones, such as amethysts, which may be picked up along the arroyos. During a trip between Sinaloa and Bamoa I picked up a handful of these stones and brought them back as souvenirs.

The gold of Jesuit days has not been exhausted in the Sierra

---

[2] There is a colonial building in Old Mesilla, New Mexico, also known today as La Posta. It was a stopping place for the stage that ran down the Old Spanish Trail into El Paso. Today, this building houses a Mexican restaurant by the name of "La Posta."

Madre Occidental; it is being profitably mined today by the San Luis Mining Company in the mountain village of Tayoltita, where all the machinery and supplies for the camp are either flown in by plane or carried over winding mountain trails on muleback. Unimportant as the sleepy village of Bamoa may be today, it was mentioned often in the official correspondence of the Jesuits when writing to their headquarters in Mexico City. The Mexican National Archives has many of these letters neatly classified, some of which give detailed information about the settlement.

Father Juan Lorenzo Salgado, in a letter to Padre Anaya, speaks of the success they were having raising cattle in 1756. He mentions nine hundred head of mules, cows, and horses. Of greater significance and arousing greater speculation is the letter telling of the inspection trip made by the famous Bishop Pedro Tamarón y Romeral in 1760. He spent a few days in Bamoa during his visit to the province of Nueva Viscaya and upon leaving made an entry in his diary saying that he would have "much more to say about this interesting village" when he returned. He continued his journey as far north as Taos, New Mexico, and returned by way of Bamoa, thereby adding one more link to the chain of circumstances binding the old settlement to the American Southwest. But although in 1765 he kept his promise to return to Bamoa, he never got to comment on it for he died upon his arrival, leaving us to conjecture as to what he might have said about the "interesting village" had he lived a little longer.

Two years after the death of Bishop Tamarón, the Jesuits suffered the worst setback in the history of the Order when, on June 25, 1767, at exactly four oclock in the morning a loud pounding was heard on the doors of the Casa Profesa, their headquarters in the Mexican capital. The insistent early callers

103

were the soldiers of Charles III, better known as Don Carlos, whose decree ordered that all members of the *Sociedad de Jesús* be taken to the ports of Veracruz on the Gulf of Mexico or Guaymas on the Gulf of California to be deported to Italy. They were not allowed to take any property along with them, and were given only enough time to pick up a few personal belongings for the journey. Father Rafael Zelis, writing years later his reminiscences of the terrible nightmare, said that they took two changes of clothing, which they rolled up into a bundle and packed on their backs. He added bitterly: "With such beautiful trappings we started the long journey."

According to Father Olmedo, librarian of the Jesuit convent recently moved from Socorro, Texas, to San Angel on the outskirts of Mexico City, the expulsion was carried out with such secrecy and thoroughness that the Jesuits had no time to think about burying or concealing anything. To my inquiry as to the probability of their having left buried the riches of which tradition speaks, he answered gravely:

"The Jesuit Order had no personal property—their vows did not permit it—and moreover, the order to leave came so unexpectedly that there was no time to conceal anything even if they had wanted to."

The scholarly padre did admit that in the interior missions the grapevine might have warned them far enough in advance to allow them time to put away whatever church property they had, hoping for their eventual return, but he added that to date nothing has been recovered. The missionaries in Bamoa and all the northern district of Sinaloa did have some time, for a year after the decree went into effect they were reported arriving at the port of Guaymas. Some inferences as to whether they had anything to leave behind may be drawn from the manner in which Father Sebastián Cava was tortured and threatened with death in the vicinity of Bamoa unless he would reveal to the soldiers who came to take him, the location of the church treasure which they insisted he had buried.

Churches all over the Hispanic world are known to have had valuables; thus it is not altogether unlikely that the church in Bamoa may have had a few items of interest to the looting soldiery. The historian Ocaranza mentions a number of valuables rescued during the flood of 1784, which destroyed the *Colegio* of Mazacori just north of Bamoa. According to him, the churchmen were able to save the "ritual vases, precious ornaments, and large quantities of silver." These precious ornaments and silver are exactly what treasure-hunters have been searching for ever since the Jesuits left the mission field.

In Bamoa there has always been a tradition that there was considerable treasure buried somewhere near the old *Colegio* or by the altar of the church built by the Jesuits; but these rumors took on more concrete form when an important document was accidentally discovered by an Indian laborer in the employ of Don Ignacio Campa, a tobacco merchant living in Sinaloa. In 1875 he sent one of his *inditos* to dig a well on the side of his property nearest the river, and by midmorning the Indian returned carrying a medium-sized rock under his arm. Don Ignacio at first thought that his servant had returned to the household for a drink of water, but his curiosity was aroused when the Indian handed him the rock saying: "Look *patrón,* what I found while digging the well."

The merchant took the rock and examined it. It was shaped like a large brick and had a sliding lid carefully fitted into a groove. The two men pried open the lid and found a wooden box inside the stone container. In the box was a yellowish roll of parchment wrapped in buckskin. Don Ignacio unrolled the important-looking document, held it flat upon the counter, and began to scan it rapidly as the Indian stood silently by. At the top was the date, 1767, followed by a careful and complete description of the location where the Jesuits of the *Colegio de Bamoa* had buried the church treasure before they were deported. A paragraph which drew Don Ignacio's attention read in part:

> In front of the pillars of the patio, facing toward the setting sun, are buried six muleloads of minted silver reales . . .

The scroll specified three additional locations where large quantities of silver and other valuables had been concealed; and stated that in the last cache the body of one of the Jesuits had been buried. The major part of the treasure was said to be buried inside the chapel in front of the altar with minute details as to its contents:

> In front of the *altar mayor* of the church, which faces the rising sun, are deposited three chandeliers of beaten gold, several chalices, a gold baptismal urn, and numerous other images . . .

The last item on the parchment was a plea to whoever should find the treasure:

> Whosoever shall uncover this treasure is requested to have Masses said for the repose of the souls of those signed below.

The rubrics of fifteen churchmen appeared at the bottom of the scroll.

The Indian laborer was rewarded for his find and sent back to finish the prosaic digging of the well, with instructions to be on the lookout for other stone containers such as the one he had just found.

There was considerable excitement in the household that evening, but it never led to action on the part of the comfortably settled merchant. Before he could make up his mind to begin the search, he was taken ill and died shortly thereafter, leaving the scroll for his three sons to think about. Only one of them took an interest in the *derrotero,* but being young, and with the family fortunes rapidly on the wane, he left the town of Sinaloa expecting to return some day to look for the treasure. No one ever learned where the father had placed the parchment, but the young son, Daniel, fortunately had committed to memory the intriguing document before it disappeared.

The intervening years dispersed the family northward, eventually to the border states of Arizona and Texas, inexorably linking the tropical town of Bamoa more closely with the Southwest. Young Daniel often thought of the treasure but a greater concern for the future led him into the Methodist ministry in Texas, where he married into a family from the same state and established still more firmly the link between the two regions.

From Marfa, Texas, the young minister and his Texan wife were sent to the mission field in Guaymas, not far enough south to bring them within searching range of the treasure, but close enough to think of the map he had committed to memory. His plan, often discussed with his wife, was to use the proceeds from Bamoa to found a model colony; and as a result of these discussions she eventually memorized the *derrotero* and became imbued with her husband's enthusiasm. From Guaymas they were assigned to La Paz in the peninsula of Lower California almost directly across from Bamoa, and by 1909 they were back at the mining town of Cananea near the border below Arizona. Then in 1910 the whole country erupted in a revolution that was to overthrow the dictator Díaz and change the course of Mexican politics, and into this upheaval the idealistic minister flung himself, hoping to help find a happier solution for the oppressed Mexican people. After four years of campaigning with the successful, though somewhat confusing revolutionaries, he was assigned to a garrison in his native Sinaloa, the very spot where he had first learned about the fabulous treasure of nearby Bamoa.

Filled with optimism at the prospect immediately before him, he wrote his wife, now back on the family ranch in Texas, of his plans to begin looking for the buried wealth. Hardly had the letter reached the family in the United States when the marauding Pancho Villa made a surprise attack upon the garrison in Sinaloa, and Daniel Campa was among those unfortunates whom he executed before fleeing back into the mountains. Thus came to a tragic end in the summer of 1914 the dream that began in 1875, in the very place where a boy had memorized the contents of a scroll now known only to a widow on a Texas ranch.

With the death of the last survivor of the original family that had learned about the treasure, the long-cherished plans to hunt for it would have vanished also, except that Daniel's widow back in Texas decided to investigate personally her husband's death. This meant that she would have to visit the village of Sinaloa across the river from the reported treasure site.

In the spring of 1916 the widow and her twelve-year-old son left Texas for the Mexican border at Nogales, Arizona, following the same route she and her husband had traveled together as missionaries at the turn of the century. When the train reached Nogales, she learned that General Mateo Muñoz, a former associate of her late husband, was somewhere below the border; and so she crossed over into Mexico in search of the General. Fortunately she overheard his name mentioned by a group of army officers riding the same train. They were on their way to attend the wedding of María Tapia and General Álvaro Obregón, the chief of the Revolution, who was later to become president of Mexico. The officers informed her that General Muñoz was back in the Sierra Madre holding the siege against an uprising of the Yaqui Indians,[3] but that his chief of staff, a General

---

[3] The Yaqui Indians have always been reluctant to submit, first to the Spaniards, and later to the Mexican government. Porfirio Díaz, the dictator,

Topete, was getting on at the next stop. When the latter was informed of the widow's mission, he placed his own car and military escort at her service and gave orders that she and her son be taken back immediately to see General Muñoz.

"Immediately" was a relative term in the days of the Mexican Revolution and particularly when it meant reaching a general deep in the rugged Sierra Madre Occidental. From the train, mother and son were transferred to a large touring car and driven across the Sonora desert until the road gave out. At this point they were met by an army vehicle equipped with solid rubber tires, with which to travel the rocky trails. The truck bounced along as far as it was possible over ravines and canyon shelves and then the passengers were transferred late at night into an army wagon pulled by two mule teams. The relay finally reached General Muñoz's headquarters at the bottom of a deep canyon.

A very surprised general greeted the young widow and her son; a woman was the last person he expected to see in the wild Indian country he was commanding. The Yaquis were entrenched in the impenetrable Bacatete Mountain and were under siege to prevent them from raiding the countryside. Soldiers were stationed every twenty paces, and from time to time replaced by other troops when the unrelenting Indians picked them off with unerring Mauser fire. Under such conditions the general hurriedly wrote letters of introduction to the military governor of Sinaloa requesting that he make available all necessary facilities to the widow of his late comrade.

Several days of travel over the Southern Pacific line brought

scattered them on ranches and haciendas through the Republic but they all found their way eventually back to Sonora, where they have their permanent habitat. The only one of the Revolutionists whom they respected was General Alvaro Obregón. He used his famous Yaqui fighters very successfully against the Díaz regime.

the lady from Texas to the city of Mazatlán where General Angel Flores the military governor was stationed. From him she received documented confirmation of her husband's death and was informed that he had been buried in the city of Sinaloa near the village of Bamoa. Mrs. Campa's desire to visit her husband's grave, and the magic name of Bamoa brought memories of plans they had discussed together. She also recalled the entire *relación* of the *derrotero* learned from her husband. The more she thought about it, the greater became her curiosity to see the treasure site. Fortunately, the military governor knew the owner of the property where the treasure was supposedly buried, and although because it was located on private property, he could not give an order authorizing her to excavate, he gave her a letter addressed to the proprietress of the land, a lady by the name of Lucia C. de Taracho, suggesting that she allow Mrs. Campa to look around the ruins of the Jesuit college. As it turned out, Señora de Taracho also knew about the treasure, and confided to the widow the circumstances under which she had acquired the land.

"For a number of years I had heard the *gente* in Sinaloa talk about a treasure which the Jesuits buried when they left Mexico, but you know, Señora, how people always talk, so I didn't pay much attention. Then one day there was a cloudburst in the mountains and the Sinaloa River came down *muy crecido*. After the water went down, someone found a number of silver reales among the mesquites where the river spilled over. That made me decide to buy the land where the ruins are located."

"You should not have gone to the military authorities about this. The two of us could handle this together easily."

Mrs. Campa asked Señora Taracho if she had ever dug for the treasure and the Mexican woman said she had done so a few years back.

"Not very long after the flood uncovered the reales, I got

some men and started digging at the west end of the ruins. We found an old tanning vat that the churchmen used for tanning hides. We also found a hand-press for coining silver reales. I sold it to a man from Mexico City who said he had a museum. Then the men uncovered a coffin with a skeleton in clerical robes! *Dios mio!* When this happened I was afraid. The men refused to dig any farther and I don't blame them. One should not disturb the dead, Señora, so I had the hole covered up again."

Mrs. Campa listened to the interesting details given by Doña Lucia but never mentioned to her the scroll found by the Indian in 1875. She was thinking that as a foreigner in a country overrun by revolution it would be advisable to contact the commander of the military garrison and be assured of something to fall back on in case she decided to dig at the ruins. He too was a general, of whom there was a great abundance in Mexico at that time. After being shown the letters Mrs. Campa had accumulated, he added one more to the collection and addressed it to the *síndico* of Bamoa. The letter read:

SINALOA, March 22, 1916

Señor Síndico de Bamoa
Bamoa
MY DEAR SIR:

This letter will be placed in your hands by Mrs. D. L. Campa who is going to Bamoa on a business which she will communicate to you personally.

I will be very grateful to you if you will assist her in every way possible. Thank you very much.

Very sincerely,
GENERAL A. NORZAGARAY

The discreet letter from the General was accompanied by another one from Señora de Taracho to her brother in Bamoa, which read:

SINALOA, March 22, 1916

Señor Gerónimo Montoya
Bamoa
DEAR GERÓNIMO:

Please tell Teófilo that Señora D. L. Campa has permission to explore around the *Casa de la Posta*.

Cordially,
LUCIA C. DE TARACHO

Note:

If the Señora hires two men, you hire two more for me, and I would advise you to have an understanding with the workers. Give them crowbars and spades.

Vale.

With these official documents Mrs. Campa arrived in Bamoa ready to begin the search. The *síndico* to whom the General's letter was addressed turned out to be a sort of village policeman, all the law that existed for the handful of people residing in Bamoa. Gerónimo Montoya was friendly and co-operative, pleased at the prospect of a treasure hunt on the family property. Word spread around immediately that a *gringa* had arrived in the village with all sorts of legal-sounding papers authorizing her to dig up the treasure near the ruins. To hear the local population talk about it, the *americana* was going to pick up several carloads of gold doubloons and cart them away like so much hay.

For the next couple of weeks everyone forgot the Revolution and gave attention to the imminent treasure hunt. This created far more excitement than they had ever had around the centuries-old Bamoa. Mrs. Campa could not begin digging until she had made a general reconnaissance of the terrain. Keeping in mind the description she had learned from her husband, she asked questions from the older residents hoping that the accumulated information might lead her to the most likely spot wherein to dig. Late one afternoon she was walking along the ruins trying to orient herself in reference to the "setting sun" mentioned in the *derrotero* of the treasure. Suddenly she realized that there was something wrong: the church faced the setting sun and not the rising sun as she had learned it from her husband. A close examination of the building didn't help much. It was old and solid, but it faced in the wrong direction. Could it be that her husband had misquoted the scroll, or had she made a mistake in recalling it? She tried to remember the wording and repeated it under her breath without hesitation:

"*In front of the* altar mayor *of the church, which faces the rising sun . . .*"

Somewhat disturbed by her discovery she returned to the house where she was staying and asked for the oldest person living in Bamoa. She was told that there was a very old woman, so old that she had to be given sips of brandy before she could speak a few words. She had no trouble locating a shrunken, wrinkled piece of humanity lying in a hammock suspended between two mesquite trees behind her great-granddaughter's *jacalito*. Her face was so covered with deep furrows and wrinkles that it was almost impossible to locate her mouth until she opened it to speak in weak and breathy whispers. Her great-granddaughter would stand over the hammock and feed her a few drops of brandy with a teaspoon, and Mrs. Campa would listen to the slow, barely audible answers she gave her questions. It was a tedious process because the old woman would become completely exhausted by her efforts to talk and fall asleep during the interrogations.

Piecing together the fragments of information the ancient gave her, Mrs. Campa learned that as a little girl, she used to play with other children, now long dead, on the ruins of the

Casa de la Posta. The foundations were then about five feet high and lay close to the south bank of the river. The structure must have been about thirty-six feet wide, and about eighty feet long, as closely as she could estimate. When asked about the church she told Mrs. Campa that it faced the setting sun, but that her grandmother used to say that the church had fallen down leaving only the back wall and the altar intact. When they rebuilt it they faced it in the opposite direction, using the back wall to save themselves the trouble of having to clear up the rubble of the old church. This was the reason it faced east instead of west.

Mrs. Campa was relieved and reassured. Knowing how most Mexican peasants felt about their churches, she thought it advisable not to try digging behind the walls of the old chapel, and so she chose a location in front of one of the pillars of the *Colegio*. Doña Lucia's brother rounded up four men, two for his sister and two for Mrs. Campa, and told them to be on hand the following day to begin digging. The sleepy village came to life on the morning when the men showed up with their spades and crowbars. They pushed importantly through the crowd of curiosity-filled adults, excited children, and women carrying babies in their *rebozos*. The entire population of Bamoa surrounded the eight-foot square selected by the lady from Texas, now referred to as *"La Texana"* among the villagers. The working men began chopping down the heavy growth of mesquite and *vinorama* and by the second day were ready to start turning up the soil.

But on that day the men stood around the clearing, showing no inclination to get to work. One of them, acting as spokesman for the group, approached Mrs. Campa and with the usual circumlocution characteristic of Mexican peasants managed to convey to her that they could not resume their work unless their wages were doubled. The Señora should understand that the *Revolución* had been a great hardship and that they had large families to feed. Mrs. Campa agreed to twice the number of pesos to get on with the digging.

The lower strata of accumulated rubbish and soil began to yield a few broken pieces of colonial pottery and other artifacts not too different from the utensils in use at Bamoa. The onlookers picked up these pieces eagerly and watched the men, expecting to see them uncover something more valuable. Every time a shovel ran into some hard object, the man at the handle would stop and look knowingly at Mrs. Campa, hoping he had struck the top of a Spanish chest. The second day ended with nothing more important than a few broken bean pots.

The third day would probably be an exciting one, and so Mrs. Campa was at the dig before the men arrived. She waited a couple of hours and still the workers had not come. By mid-morning one of them, the one who had asked for the raise, appeared without his tools and with a shrug of the shoulders announced to his boss that *"Siempre no,"* which meant that they had changed their minds. The widow tried to learn the reason, but all she got was more shoulder shrugs and evasive answers. Finally he suggested that maybe if she doubled their pay, which already had been doubled, they might return. Mrs. Campa thought it over and decided that having come this far she might as well meet their demands and continue the digging.

It soon became apparent to her that the search was going to become increasingly expensive at the rate the wages were rising. She was at the mercy of simple-minded folk who merely shrugged their shoulders when she tried to reason with them. Their reluctance was not altogether unwillingness to work, but a vague resentment caused by the presence of an outsider, an interloper who was going to carry away a treasure that belonged to them. To make matters worse, rumors began to filter down to the little town about an incident that had taken place early in March of the same year. Pancho Villa had raided Columbus,

New Mexico, and there was talk of retaliation by the American Army. This meant *intervención,* a word that fired the already aroused Mexicans with nationalistic feelings.

The talk about a possible conflict between Mexico and the United States brought the excavation at Bamoa to a standstill, and the Texas widow began to fear that it might be inadvisable for a foreigner to remain so far in the interior of Mexico when conditions were getting tense. She began to think about the children she had left in Texas, and before very long she realized that her anxiety to return home was stronger than her desire to continue searching for a Jesuit treasure. She hired a conveyance to take her across the river to Sinaloa and immediately began preparations to return.

In a few days a train with the usual military escort of Revolutionary days was to start moving toward the border, and the military commander arranged for passage and a *salvo conducto* to take the widow and her son across the embattled lines of northwest Mexico. Her friends in Sinaloa helped with provisions for the long trip by presenting her with several aged cheeses, *quesos añejos,* for which Sinaloa is justly famous. As it turned out, these heavy cheeses became the source of considerable speculation among those who knew that she had been digging for a treasure in Bamoa. The porters who lifted her suitcases, heavy with cheese, raised their eyebrows and exclaimed, "Caramba!" One of her late husband's friends who accompanied her to the railroad station whispered discreetly in her ear: "Please, señora, just one *antigua* for a souvenir!" The more Mrs. Campa tried to explain, the more convinced everyone became that she was loaded with gold from Bamoa.

The first day on the train revealed the same misconjecture. It was customary for trains during the Mexican Revolution to travel only in the daytime because they were easier targets under cover of dark. The passengers found lodging in whatever town they happened to reach at nightfall, and boarded the train again the following morning. On the first evening of her return trip, Mrs. Campa was trying to make herself and her young son as comfortable as she could in the none-too-modern coaches, when the conductor approached her, saying:

"Pardon me, señora, but you are not safe here tonight. Every one knows that you are carrying valuables and someone might disturb you."

She insisted that she had nothing of consequence with her, other than a few personal belongings, whereupon the conductor lowered his voice and spoke in confidential tones: "Yes, I understand, but you see, the . . . *tesoro* in your suitcases."

As he said this he turned his eyes significantly toward the suitcases between the seats. Again Mrs. Campa tried to tell him that all she had was aged cheeses, but she finally decided to find a room in town for the sake of her son and the safety of her *quesos añejos*.

Mrs. Campa left Sinaloa with a few more documents and with a deeper conviction that the *derrotero* uncovered by the Indian was more than a mere curiosity. She felt frustrated in her attempt to find the treasure, and promised herself to return when things quieted down in Mexico. Meanwhile she confided part of the story to an old family friend in the city of Mazatlán by the name of Ramón Maldonado y Osuna. He wrote regularly to her and in the early thirties suggested that they go in together and buy an "instrument for locating mineral deposits," which had just appeared on the market. Later on he negotiated with a German firm for this scientific doodlebug and on April 24, 1935 wrote the following enthusiastic letter to Mrs. Campa, who by then had moved to Albuquerque, New Mexico:

I have secured the instrument I told you about in my previous correspondence and am ready to begin operations any time you decide. All you need to do is wire me: 'I am on my way' and I'll join you in Bamoa.

Shortly thereafter he wrote again saying that he had suffered a minor accident from which he hoped to recover in a matter of weeks. The silence that followed indicated that Don Ramón had written his last letter.

CHAPTER 9

THE AUTHOR BECOMES INVOLVED

◆

THE STORY of the Jesuit treasure of Bamoa had fascinated me
when I first heard my mother's account of her unsuccessful attempt to search for it during the Mexican Revolution days,
and her inability to carry out her original plan made me feel that
the story was still incomplete. I wanted to know whether the
parchment found by the Indian digging the well really led to
muleloads of coined silver, and in the back of my mind I harbored a very strong hope of going down to Bamoa some day to
look for the hoard.

The long process of growing up, years of schooling, and two
world wars took place before I could make definite plans to investigate this legend, which had been in our family for three
generations. Upon my return from Europe at the end of World
War II, I began to study the early history of Bamoa, and in the
course of my investigation contacted a man by the name of Filiberto Quintero, who was working on the history of El Fuerte,
a region adjoining the treasure site. He informed me that so far
as he knew the Jesuit treasure had never been found. During our
exchange of correspondence I learned also that he was the state
treasurer of Sinaloa and therefore could help me make whatever
arrangements were necessary.

As it turned out, there was no need for anything except

dry weather, and this commonly occurred during the winter months; and so in mid-December I left Denver with the entire family to take a tour along the west coast of Mexico. We drove down to Albuquerque and turned southwest on Highway 80 at Hatch, New Mexico. On the third day we reached the border city of Nogales, Arizona, and crossed over into the state of Sonora, reaching Hermosillo, the capital, the same day late in the afternoon after a very interesting drive through the stately organ cactus and the ghostly saguaros. In Hermosillo I looked up Professor Pesqueira of the Anthropology Department of the state university to get further firsthand information about the Jesuit missions of northern Sinaloa near Bamoa. From him I learned that the west coast Pan American Highway was not yet open much farther than Guaymas. This meant that the family would have to lie over in Hermosillo while I continued the rest of the way to Culiacán by plane to meet Señor Quintero. There was some disappointment at this change of plans, but the friendliness of the people in Hermosillo, the orange groves heavy with fruit, and the balmy winter weather compensated in part for the separation.

The air trip to Culiacán was made interesting by the reception given at every stop along the way. There were a number of baseball players of the Mexican Western League going down to join their respective teams in the larger cities like Mazatlán and Guadalajara, and the fans were on hand at every airport to greet them.

Don Filiberto Quintero, whom I met for the first time, proved to be a well-informed man and a genial host with an extensive library, which he placed at my disposal the day I arrived. My original plan to reach Bamoa by land had to be abandoned because of an unseasonable rainstorm in the northern Sierras; and the Southern Pacific Railroad, recently acquired by the Mexican government, had as yet no fixed schedule. There was, however, a northbound plane flight that stopped once a week at a small village named Guasave whenever there were passengers or mail to pick up. From this village I could hire a car to drive me to Bamoa, twenty-five miles distant, provided the Sinaloa River was not swollen by the rains. There being no flight that I could take for the next three days, Señor Quintero and I spent several pleasant afternoons at the extremely popular baseball games, and some entertaining evenings at the city's Casino, a club where the leading families dined, wined, and amused themselves at late dinners in animated conversation under the historical *"Portales"* of Culiacán.

On the day I was to leave for Guasave, I took a taxi to the airport, expecting to start early in the morning and possibly have my first look at Bamoa before the end of the day. Unfortunately, the plane I was to take blew a tire upon landing and had to lie over until a replacement arrived from Mexico City on another flight. During the long wait I became acquainted with a very talkative and friendly Nestle Company salesman who assumed that I too was representing some American firm. In the customary way of travelers, we began trading impressions about the places we had been, during which I mentioned that Guasave was my next stop.

"You may have been in worse places, *amigo,* but you will find Guasave unique," my friend remarked.

That sounded interesting, and so I asked him to recommend a place to stay.

"I think that since you've never been to Guasave you should stop at *La Casa de la Güera,* he answered."

I was about to question him further about his recommendation when my plane was announced, and so we simply shook hands and said *Adiós.* A couple of hours after we took off, the steward came over to notify me that we were landing in Guasave. All I could see from the plane was a pasture with a very small structure alongside of a barely outlined strip. The wheels touched the runway and the plane taxied to the "airport" where it paused long enough for the steward to hand me my bag and wave a friendly "*Adiós.*" It was a new sensation to be delivered, bag in hand, into the middle of the tropics like a milk can on a rural route; quite a departure from the usual noise of loud-speakers, porters hustling around, and taxi drivers looking for fares. At a glance I took in all there was to the "airport," including a car parked in the shade of a large mesquite tree. I walked over to it and noticed a man at the wheel, who answered my greeting and asked if I wanted a ride into town. I accepted the invitation, threw my bag in the back seat, climbed in with the driver, and asked him to take me to a hotel.

"There's only one hotel in town, señor, but if you wish, I can take you over to *La Casa de la Güera,* where most people usually stop in Guasave."

This was the second recommendation I had been offered about a stopping place in Guasave, and it made me wonder if it were really the best or the one to which salesmen and taxi drivers connived to send travelers. I turned the thought over in my mind several times before I decided in roulette-wheel fashion to try the hotel.

From my driver, whose name was Vicente Angulo, I learned that Bamoa was about an hour's drive from Guasave, and that he could take me there provided I could wait until the following morning. There being no fixed rates, Vicente and I went through the interesting Mexican sport of bargaining until we bested each other by agreeing on forty pesos for the trip and five more for every additional hour spent in Bamoa.

The tropical sun was setting when we arrived in Guasave, a small village with dusty streets, flat-covered colonial houses, and an air of peaceful existence of a more factual than descriptive sort. Vicente stopped the car in front of a building that seemed in the process of construction, although most of the process had apparently stopped many years before when the builder changed his mind and failed to finish the ground floor.

"Here's the hotel, señor," he announced. All I could see was an ancient truck parked inside of what eventually could be a doorway, provided that door frames and doors should be installed. Behind the truck was a stack of straw surrounded by a miscellaneous assortment of chickens scratching around optimistically on the ground. Farther back was a flight of wooden stairs like those improvised ladders put up by plasterers during construction. Unable to see any hotel sign I turned to Vicente and asked:

"Just where is the entrance to this hotel?"

He pointed to the stairs I had been surveying and explained that the hotel was on the second story, or what appeared to be the roof. The owner, I was told later, ran short of funds when he was constructing the building and decided to finish the second floor first in order to earn some income. Reassured that I had reached *the* hotel in town, I climbed the stairs and came to a landing with a row of rooms on the far side and a shed-like construction adjoining it that displayed a rather imposing sign: *ADMINISTRACIÓN*. Under the sign was a row of long keys to match the rooms. As I approached the counter a woman who had been bending over a washtub, straightened up, wiped her hands on her apron, and greeted me. To my request for the best room in the house she answered apologetically:

"I'm sorry, señor, but the roof fell in on the room that had bed-springs. The best one is Number 9, and it's not occupied."

I entered my name on the register and took the key to Number 9. It was a long room with a small window high up on the back wall. In the corner below the window was an old-fashioned canvas cot almost three feet high. The table in the middle of the room and the chair to match it were the only other pieces of furniture, but the most intriguing equipment was installed behind a partial wall separating the bath from the rest of the room. There were two fixtures. One was a water pipe along the wall bent down gooseneck fashion for those who could manage a shower by balancing themselves on two loose tiles over a sewer opening on the floor. The other installation had a sign above it which read:

> Guests are requested to dispose of soiled paper in the waste basket in order not to stop up the plumbing.

These conveniences were what made Number 9 the choice room in the hotel.

After resting for awhile on the *catre de tijera,* as the high canvas cots are called, I went down to look for a place to eat. The lady at the ADMINISTRACIÓN recommended a very good restaurant across the street where they sold *"comida muy sabrosa."* I decided to try out this place where the food was so tasty. It was a sidewalk cafe extending halfway to the street and protected from the traffic by a low picket fence. You could wave at your friends as they went by on a donkey or in a car. The arrangement, I must admit, was a great idea socially, but I was looking for something with a little more privacy. As I approached the entrance I noticed two young men talking to the proprietress. One had a sample case in his hand and the other was apparently filling out an order. When they were through, I asked them:

"Pardon me, *señores,* can either of you tell me where I can find a good restaurant?"

With the easy nonchalance common to salesmen, one of the young men answered:

"We can't recommend a *good* restaurant, but if you care to share with us the lesser of two evils we suggest you join us at *La Casa de la Güera* where we are stopping."

124

No matter where I went or to whom I talked, I was inexorably destined to patronize *La Güera*,[1] and as by now I was really curious to find out what this place known as "Blondie's" was like I accepted the invitation. We stumbled along over the upturned cobblestones in the dark street until we reached a dimly lighted doorway, which in colonial days must have been the *zaguán* of the house for carriages to drive through to the interior patio. The entrance led into such a patio, now converted into a combination kitchen and dining room with a long table in the center and a row of charcoal *braseros* along the wall where the *tortilleras* were baking corn *tortillas* over cast iron *comales*. The other sides of the quadrangle led to the rooms occupied by traveling salesmen and other transients who stopped at *La Güera's* popular pension in Guasave.

My new acquaintances invited me to their quarters where I noticed that they too had tall canvas cots like the one in Number 9 at the hotel. An Indian girl was filling a pitcher of water at the washstand, and as she walked out threw a community towel over the back of one of the chairs with the suggestion that the señores could go into the dining room any time they felt like it. In a few minutes we heard a pleasant contralto calling: *"Listo! Servidos! A cenar!"*

Supper was being served on the long table in the middle of the patio presided over by a middle-aged woman, who obviously was trying to hold on to her obsolescent good looks. She greeted us with a pleasant *"Buenas Noches"* as we sat down. This was *"La Güera,"* a plump but well-proportioned blondish

[1] Contrary to popular belief, Latin Americans have always been sensitive to color shades. In colonial times there were nineteen designations for the mixtures of Indian, Negro, and White. The term *güero* comes from the word *huero* meaning not well done. It is applied to an egg that is halfway between being fresh and hatched. In Mexico it simply means "blonde," and in many places where a non-Indian is an exception, the term is applied even to persons who by European standards would hardly qualify as blondes.

woman, whose reputation had probably been made before she opened the pension that bore her name. She was good-natured and could keep up her end of the picaresque banter to which the salesmen subjected her throughout the meal, smiling ruefully at the salty jokes of her uproarious customers.

The same maid who a few moments before had brought water into the rooms came to take orders for drinks. It was either milk or coffee. Before I could express my choice, one of the customers volunteered: "Order milk if you wish; they boil it here." I was thankful for the tip, but just then I preferred a cup of very hot coffee. A second waitress came in with a pile of corn *tortillas* on a plate, dealing them out like cards at a poker game: five to a customer. Each tortilla hand fell on a tablecloth of the same greyish color on the customer's right, and when all had been served the girl went back to bring fried meat, fried beans, potatoes, and sliced tomatoes, which were placed in the middle of the table in time-honored boardinghouse style. For dessert we were served canned peaches, courtesy of my travelling salesmen friends, who took a mock bow when *La Güera* gave them a half-humorous, half-courteous acknowledgment.

"Blondie's" establishment was picturesque and in a way reminiscent of one of those inns described by Cervantes in *Don Quixote*. The long table, the dim light, the charcoal stoves, maids dealing out *tortillas,* dogs hopefully expecting a bone under the table, and *La Güera* herself standing with her arms crossed always ready with a sharp retort. The "lesser of two evils," as it had been described earlier in the evening, had proved to be far more interesting than the sidewalk cafe across the street from my hotel, but since I had been given the best room in the house I had no alternative but to return reluctantly to Number 9 that night.

Surprisingly enough, the canvas cot was quite comfortable, and despite the excitement over the anticipated trip to Bamoa, I was able to sleep until the defiant crowing of the fighting cocks in the yard awakened me. I decided to make as much use as possible of the conveniences provided by the *ADMINISTRA-CIÓN* at the hotel, and thoroughly refreshed I walked back to *La Güera's* for another of her home-cooked meals. This being breakfast, she had added fried eggs to the menu of the preceding evening. I ordered *huevos rancheros* on toasted *tortillas* not only to vary the diet but also because they are very tasty served with a dash of hot sauce. It was a substantial breakfast and one that would have to hold me until we returned from Bamoa.

Vicente and I had agreed to leave at about eight-thirty, but being in the tropics I did not expect him to show up much before nine. It was therefore a surprise to find him waiting for me at the hotel when I returned, ready to take me on the last lap of an expedition, which was made more exciting by my Mexican driver.

Vicente was a cross between a race driver and a bullfighter when he was at the wheel. As soon as we were out of town he swung the car into a set of deep-worn ruts over a loose gravel bed with a dangerous-looking high center, but he drove so fast that he literally skimmed over the center ridge. He was hurrying through "the good part of the road," so he explained, because further on we should have to slow down for the *columpios* on the highway. I was wondering what his interpretation of "slow" over the coming dips would be when he caught up with another speeding car trailing a thick cloud of dust. In one operation, Vicente swung the car to the left, stepped on the gas, and bounced right back into the ruts in the center of the road after he passed the other car. I didn't know whether to praise him or censure him for the feat.

Hardly had we settled back on the road when I noticed a young Indian driving a string of donkeys loaded with straw not very far ahead of us. All but one of his moving haystacks had got safely across, and the boy was trying frantically to persuade the last one to cross the highway before we caught up with them, but the *burrito* stood his ground and merely turned his head aside as Vicente's car rushed by without slackening its speed. All I could do was to get into the spirit of the sport and shout "Ole!" like a good fan. There was still more excitement for us before we reached the dips, which were to diminish our speed to Vicente's version of slow. The culverts and short bridges on the road had never been installed. I looked with apprehension at the first one we came to when I noticed that there were only two wooden planks laid across the ditch for us to drive over. As we flew safely across I asked Vicente, "Ever miss one of these?" to which he answered casually: "No, señor, one gets used to it."

The dips were every bit of the *columpios* he had said they would be, but out of consideration for me Vicente slowed down enough to keep me from literally hitting the roof. After a few more miles of this rhythmic driving we reached a clearing through the *vinorama* and mesquites along the Sinaloa River, where mule drivers and cowherds forded the stream. According to Vicente, Bamoa was just on the other side, but we could not see it through the heavy growth of bushes and trees. At the sloping bank of the ford, he eased the car gently into the current and started across with such confidence that when the water reached the floor boards I was completely unconcerned. Vicente, with his customary calm, noticed the rising water line and remarked: "Must have rained in the sierras today."

Just as we reached dry land on the opposite side, the engine died. There was nothing further to do but wait until the coils dried enough to start again; I was destined to reach my objective in short, uneasy stages. With nothing but time on our hands, Vicente and I tried to be good company to each other, and as the conversation progressed he became curious to know why I had come to this out-of-the-way village. This subject led naturally to stories about treasures, of which my traveling companion had a good store for me to listen to.

"Oh, *si*, there are many *tesoros* all over this country. The last one I know about was found a few miles south of Guasave on the Pan American Highway. I had a friend who ran a bulldozer for the *Empresa* building the road, and one day while he was digging the roadbed his blade turned up a big rawhide *talega* filled with gold coins, old Spanish *monedas de oro*. He got so excited that he left the dulldozer standing right where he found the gold and started for Mexico City. Later on I learned that he had taken an *autobus* in Culiacán after buying new clothes and having some fun in the city. He never has returned to Aluey."

I tried to turn his attention to the ruins in Bamoa but Vicente was more interested in what had happened on the coast, and for a very good reason. He had been looking for the treasure of *Los Piratas de los Pozos* on the seashore town by the same name. "Have you ever heard tell," he asked me, "of this pirate treasure?" I asked him to tell the story.

"It is not a story, señor, it's the truth. A lot of gold coins have been found on the beach where the pirates were killed. In the colonial epoch there was a pirate who roamed all over the Gulf of California raiding the seaport towns like Guaymas and Mazatlán. The Spanish navy tried to capture this ship but it always eluded them until one day two warships spied him on the high seas west of La Punta de San Ignacio and cut off his escape.

"When the pirates saw that they could not get back to *altamar* they headed their ship for the coast and beached it near a town called Los Pozos. By the time the sailors came on shore, the pirates had hidden their cargo of gold and jewels so well that no trace of it could be found. The Spanish captain hanged those who were not killed in the battle because they would not tell him where they had hidden the treasure.

"About ten years ago there was a big storm at sea and the waves tore loose many *barrancos* along the shore. After the storm was over, the people from Aluey and Los Pozos went over to see the damage and found some old coins washed on shore, and also skeletons and bones of the pirates who had died in battle. Since that time people go to the beaches of Los Pozos looking for coins. I have gone several times and dug around with my friends, but all we have found is bones."

Vicente tried the starter again, and as the engine came to life he closed the story with the remark:

"Some day, believe me, someone will find the treasure!"

We were now on the last lap of the trip, actually within hogcalling distance of my objective. The trail from the river bank where we had stalled, wound around a thick growth of thorny mesquite and the ever-present *vinorama* tree. It suddenly opened into a flat space covered with two rows of tropical *jacales*. At the far end of what might be termed the village main street stood the church, much too tall for the cluster of slant-roofed, mud-plastered shacks that surrounded it. When we came to the first house, I asked Vicente to stop while I walked over to a man standing in the doorway.

"Buenos días, señor, I wonder if you can tell me the location of some old ruins known as *La Casa de la Posta*," I inquired.

With undisguised curiosity visible in his eyes, but with the accustomed courtesy of Mexican villagers, the man answered:

"No, señor, I can't tell you. I've only been here for the past ten years, but the man at the store across the street should know; he is from here."

The man at the little store had heard his neighbor's reference to him and was ready to be of service to me. We greeted each other as I entered the door, and before I could ask him he volunteered:

"You're the one who is looking for the ruins, no? I can

point them out to you but it is better that you go to the barber farther on. The ruins are behind his house along a little pathway not very far from the road."

We drove down the street until we came to another *jacalito* with an open front where a man was bending over a customer reclining in a barber's chair. The barber looked up as the car stopped before his shop. Simultaneously the customer sat up, surprised to see a car in Bamoa. His whiskers were so long that the barber was using hand clippers before shaving him, and had finished only one side of his face when we arrived. Like the other Bamoans I had talked to, the barber was not shy and appeared less hesitant in answering my questions than I was in asking them.

"Oh *sí, cómo no!*" He knew how to get to the ruins behind the shop and started to point with his clippers, but decided to take me there personally and introduce me to the old ladies who lived on the property. I insisted that he should not let me inter-rupt his work, but both he and his customer assured me that they would be happy to show me the way *con mucho gusto.* With the barber in the lead and his half-shaved customer behind, we proceeded toward the ruins along the pathway back of the shop. Vicente brought up the rear in the company of the curious children, who had joined us, eager to learn what the strangers were doing at the old Jesuit ruins.

We emerged from the path into a small patio formed by a mud-plastered *jacal* on either side and a low thick wall which seemed to keep the tangle of weeds from crowding into the patio. Cuca and Gonzaga López lived in one of these *jacalitos* where the barber knocked. Both old women came out and were introduced.

"Doña Cuca," said the barber, "here is a gentleman who would like to speak to you."

The barber went on to tell them by way of introduction

that the señor was looking for the ruins of *La Casa de la Posta*. Cuca, who was the spokesman for the two, lost no time in telling me that the wall upon which I was leaning was part of the Jesuit ruins I had come to see. The land beyond the wall was so over-grown with vegetation that I hadn't noticed how far the remains of the ancient structure extended. As closely as I could make out, the building must have been about eighty or a hundred feet long by about forty wide. Doña Cuca explained to me that this was not the complete building but only the north wing of the court-yard. In my mind I visualized the *portales* and the *pilares* men-tioned in the legend and wondered at the foot of which one of these were the "muleloads of silver coins." Not far from the patio where we were standing there was an excavation about six feet deep and ten feet across, partly covered with growth. I asked Doña Cuca about it and she launched into a story about a *gran señora* who had been there during the *Revolución*.

"She was an elegant lady with gloves and hat, who came to Bamoa one day many years ago. She had official papers and documents with which to dig for the treasure and hired a num-ber of men to dig for her. We never found out what she took out because one day she disappeared and never came back again, but they say that she had her suitcases full of gold."

I began to wonder if anyone else besides the "elegant lady" had come to search for the treasure and asked Doña Cuca about it. She mentioned a method used by a treasure-hunting Spaniard, which reminded me of the water witches of Texas.

"There was a man, a Spaniard, who said he had read about the treasure back in Spain. He had with him a *peso cacique* tied with a piece of string. He drew an arrow pointing out of the center of the peso and wound up the string which he held in his hand tight. He let the coin dangle by the string and then let it unwind. He did this several times and each time the arrow on the peso pointed to the base of that mesquite you see in the middle of the patio."

Both sisters were positive that the treasure was still there and continued to give additional evidence to prove it. A woman in the crowd of bystanders, holding a baby in her arms, prompted Cuca:

"Doña Cuca, tell the señor about the woman dressed in white who appears each month."

The old lady moistened her lips with her tongue and began the story:

"Every month when the moon is in *creciente* a beautiful woman dressed in white robes appears on the wall behind where you are now standing, steps down gently into the patio, and begins to walk slowly around the mesquite tree. She keeps her eyes directly on the base of the tree and never utters a word. The first night I saw her, I ran into the house calling on the saints, but both my sister Gonzaga and I watched her from the window until she disappeared back into the ruins. Ask the neighbors—they've seen her too."

There was a chorus of assent from the people gathered in the patio. According to them, the apparition was so regular that they had become accustomed to it, and simply watched the woman walk her rounds until she disappeared behind the wall.

The last person who had come looking for the treasure was an *americano*. He spent several days during World War II searching with an instrument, which from the description given I took to be some sort of electronic device for locating metals. He wanted to dig but they would not let him, and so he eventually went away. Finally I brought up the subject of digging and was given an enthusiastic approval by both sisters:

"Señor, why don't you start digging tomorrow? You can bring American machines and dig up the tree. There is a treasure here left by the Jesuits, but what can two old ladies do? We don't even own a shovel!"

I pointed out to them that their little *jacalitos* would be in the way of the excavation, but they answered in chorus:

"*Que importa,* señor! Knock them down and we'll build them out of the way farther back. Only one thing we ask: when you get the treasure, we want to have enough of it to visit the capital. They say that Mexico City is a beautiful place and we want to see it before we die. That's all we want; you can have the rest."

As I listened to their entreaties I wondered if they were not thinking of the old tradition held by Mexicans who claim that anyone who dies without seeing the capital will turn over in his grave.

There was still one detail about the legend that needed looking into. The *derrotero* said that the church was supposed to face the rising sun, and in actuality it faced in the opposite direction. After taking leave of my two informants at the ruins, I walked over to the church, but instead of going in I went around to the back wall to look for a rectangle where I was told nothing grew. That part of the church property had been put to such regular use by the inhabitants of Bamoa for so many years that it was difficult to determine whether the barrenness of the place was due to these abuses or to some other natural cause. At any rate, it soon became clear to me that there was only one way to find out how accurate were the directions given in the parchment found by the Indian who dug a well for Don Ignacio in 1875, and that was to dig. That thought was in my mind when I drove back to Guasave with Vicente, where I boarded the plane that took me back to the twentieth century.

CHAPTER 10

The lost dupont mine

◆

THE PROSPECTOR had a conscience, but it took a long time for it to move him enough to confess to a crime he committed back in 1884. It was not until 1900 that F. D. Thompson decided to tell the truth about what happened to his one-time mining partner, Harris Dupont, while they were working on a claim in northern New Mexico. Thompson's idea of a confession was simply to write a succinct account of what he claimed happened and then turn the story over to the first clergyman he came across. Thus when he saw a priest crossing the road to Alameda, eight miles north of Albuquerque, he spurred his horse to meet him.

The good padre was the parish priest who ministered to the scattered *ranchitos* that comprised the village of Alameda at the turn of the present century. One day, very early in the morning, he started to cross the road from his church, when he heard hoofbeats. He stopped, looked down the road, and noticed a man riding toward him at full gallop. He waited for the rider to pass by, but to his surprise, instead of going on the man brought the horse to a stop directly in front of him, leaned over the saddle, and handed him an envelope saying, "I'm glad to get this off my chest!" With this cryptic comment he dug the spurs into his mount and disappeared along the narrow wagon road that one had been part of the Old Spanish Trail.

The priest had an urgent matter to attend to just then at the home of a rancher by the river, who had a dying son badly gored by a range bull; therefore he slipped the letter into his pocket and hurried on to his mission. "Probably another contribution by some repentant sinner who is trying to make amends for his misdeeds," he thought. The sinner could wait, and so the padre walked on.

The events of the morning so occupied the padre's thoughts that he did not remember the letter until he returned to his room about noon and removed his coat. Then he took it out, broke open the envelope, and was surprised not to find the contribution he had expected from the rider's remark upon leaving. The thickness of the enclosure was due to a two-page account poorly scribbled in English accompanied by two maps, one an improvised pencil-drawing giving the contours and landmarks of some site back in the mountains by Cuba, New Mexico, and the other a marked copy of a regular United States map. The opening paragraph read:

> In the name of our Lord I want to make this true confession and to my best and honest truth I tell you father that for the last sixteen years my conscience has troubled me—that for sure I have to tell the truth."

With this unliterary introduction, the writer went into a somewhat detailed account of what he had done, being careful to present his side of the story in such a way as to give him some degree of justification for his deed.

It seems that in the early spring of 1879 he had met a man by the name of Harris Dupont at a cantina in El Paso. After a few drinks the two became better acquainted with each other and found out in the course of their conversation that both had the same interest: prospecting for gold, although Dupont who was a good deal older than Thompson was considerably more experienced.

A few days after their initial meeting, Dupont suggested to young Thompson that they throw in together and try their luck in New Mexico, where there were signs of some promise reported by mining men returning to El Paso. This was just what the young prospector hoped his newly made friend would suggest; he wanted to pair up with someone who knew the country well, and Harris Dupont seemed to be just the man. Together they bought two stout Sonoran burros, which they loaded with gear and supplies, and in a few days they were up in the Organ Mountains trying their luck. Most of the good locations had already been taken; after an unsuccessful week they pulled up stakes and decided to look around in the Magdalena Mountains west of Socorro.

Dupont suggested to Thompson that they follow the Spanish Trail over the Jornada del Muerto as far as Fort Craig and then take the canyon mule trail between the two mountain ranges in order to save at least five days' to a week's travel. The old Jornada was not used a great deal at that time except by those who could travel fast, but since all the two miners were carrying was their gear on two large burros they decided on this route. In order to make sure of their water supply they traded for two small Mexican casks and filled them just before they started up the trail above their Organ Mountains claim.

Magdalena was still not what Dupont was searching for; accordingly after a month in this region he and his partner turned east until they reached the Spanish Trail again and then continued northward through Albuquerque to the village of Bernalillo. Here they learned about a good-sized operation that was going on in the Gallina Mountains near Cuba. The reports they heard sounded as though this was what they were looking for, but these word-of-mouth reports proved to be greatly exaggerated. They had expected to find a smelter at Copper City, as the place was euphemistically called, but all they found was a job. As their funds were almost exhausted by now, they joined the outfit as pick-and-shovel miners. Dupont, because of his experience, was paid regular wages, but Thompson, who was still a beginner, was paid a dollar and a half a day. It was enough to live on and save a small amount. The job included board also, and as for "room," they had their own tent and bed-rolls.

Harris Dupont was not altogether disappointed, and he told Thompson that with a little prospecting in his spare time they might find a location that would pay a lot more than wages. He began to roam over the adjoining mountains and sometimes stayed longer than he had expected, but he always explained his overdue absences by claiming to have got lost or taken ill while hiking.

One day Dupont told his partner after one of his long week-end prospecting expeditions that he had found a place where they could hit a rich lode that would set them up independently. According to his story, the place he had in mind was up past the village of Cuba in San Pedro Park. Thompson agreed to give it a try, for he too was weary of being a day laborer. The two were careful to save as much of their earnings as they possibly could, and within a month they decided to strike out on their own. They outfitted themselves anew, purchased additional mining tools, loaded a good supply of grub on their burros, which had grown fat from grazing along the slopes near the camp, and left Copper City. Now that they were going to work their own claim together the two prospectors made a formal partnership in which they agreed to share proportionately.

Dupont led the way into the mountains and chose a campsite centrally located in the region they were to prospect. He did not take long to find what he was looking for, and Thompson in his "Confession" was eloquent about their strike:

> Finally one day we hit a ridge on the west slope of the mountains. This is, I believe, one of the richest gold lodes in the territory of New Mexico.

They moved their camp and pitched a new one near the mouth of their newly-opened mine, and as they approached from the back side of the hill where the ground sloped more gradually they came upon a spring of water. Their luck had finally changed, for now they could set up sluice boxes, begin washing the ore, and recover gold dust as well. Thompson continued his narrative by saying that in a few weeks they had accumulated a good batch of gold and stored it in their tent. As the quantity increased, they began to worry for fear someone would come by while they were at the mine; therefore they took their gold and rode their burros down to Lagunitas, about fifteen miles from camp, to a store run by a Jewish merchant named Matheus or Mathias, Thompson was not sure in his account. Dupont, who was the senior partner, made arrangements for the merchant to buy their gold every week thereafter. He gave Thompson a twenty-dollar gold coin for every week they had worked, and continued this practice from then on.

All went well for the first year; twenty dollars was a considerable increase from the dollar and a half a day Thompson had been getting at Copper City as a hired laborer. But then he began to have doubts about the transaction that took place every Saturday at the Jewish merchant's general store. He never mentioned anything to Dupont but decided to work things out for himself somehow. One part of this weekly routine that began to arouse his suspicion was that Dupont usually disappeared casually from camp on Saturday evenings after returning from the store.

One night when they came back from their trading expedition, Thompson decided to follow his partner and try to find out where he went so late at night. After snuffing out the candles, Dupont instead of turning in for the night walked out of the tent fully dressed. Thompson crawled behind him on all fours and followed him from a safe distance. He could see Dupont silhouetted against the night sky. Walking up the mountain slope from camp, he stood quiet for a short while, seemed to be looking around to make sure that he was alone, then walked briskly through the pine trees. By now, Thompson was able to follow under cover of the forest and watch the other's movements. Dupont entered a thick clump of scrub oak, bent down and stayed in that position for a good while, and then retraced his steps and headed back to camp.

Thompson waited until his partner was out of sight and then went over to the scrub oak clump where he had seen him disappear. By parting the brush with his hands he came to a small clearing. In the dark he felt around on the ground and discovered a rock under a thin layer of soft earth. He promptly moved the rock and found an opening of considerable size, about eighteen inches below the surface. He put his hand into the opening and felt the cold but pleasant contact of gold coins. He reached farther with both hands and realized that he had come upon a cache of greater proportions than he had anticipated. Dupont had been hoarding the gold they had been mining for over a year, except for the twenty-dollar piece he gave him as his share every Saturday night.

Thompson stated in the account given to the priest just how he felt:

> I confess to you father that right there I had my first bad impression of my partner.

This was an understatement, for Thompson became so upset that he actually got sick. When he came back into the tent, Dupont had lighted a candle and was looking for him. As he entered, Dupont noticed the expression on his face and asked him, "What's the matter, Tony? Are you sick?"

Tony *was* sick. He was sick to learn that for over a year he had been getting twenty dollars a week while his partner, who was supposed to share proportionately with him, was probably getting fifty times twenty and hiding it for a purpose he had never disclosed to the man who was his friend and working partner. Thompson didn't know what to answer at the moment; he made up something that would hold until he could collect his thoughts.

"No, I'm not sick; I'm worried about that drill we bought at the store today. I hope it's not as soft as the last one we bought."

This seemed to satisfy Dupont, who for a moment had imagined that his partner had found him out. They talked about the relative merits of steel drills for awhile and decided to try out the new one the next morning.

No matter when they went to bed, Thompson and Dupont always rose early, and this morning was no different from any other. After washing the dishes, they took the drill, and went out to a large rock at the opening of the mine just a few paces from camp. Harris Dupont held the drill with both hands while Thompson pounded it with an eight-pound sledge hammer. As he looked down at his partner's profile, whose hands were occupied holding the drill, he was still thinking of the pittance he was receiving as his share of what had now increased to a very profitable enterprise.

He wondered if this were the opportune moment to bring up the subject, but he rejected the idea immediately. Dupont would guess that he had been spying on him and this would probably lead to unpleasantness. With each blow of the hammer he tried to think of a way to begin; and the more he thought about

it the more his temper mounted, until blinded by the realization
that he had been cheated by his partner for many years, he deflect-
ed the next blow and brought down the hammer on the top of
Dupont's head. Before he could realize what he was doing, he

142

had angrily dealt his partner a second blow and left him lying where he fell. He slung the hammer away into the brush and walked back to camp, where he remained dazed and confused for the rest of the day.

Before sundown, Thompson dragged Dupont's body up the trail and threw it into the brush where it would not be completely hidden and yet not too easily discovered. He went back to the gold cache he had found the night before, looked at the large pile of coins Dupont had accumulated, and put a few handfuls in his pockets. He was totally lost now that he had no one with whom to go back into the mine. The daily routine had become so much a part of his living that without it he became disoriented. Gradually, as his anger subsided he began to feel the remorse of a man who had acted on impulse and was not by nature a killer. In the letter to the priest he explained his deed very briefly: "His intention was to rob me and I could not control my temper."

For two days he stayed in camp wondering what to do. Finally he decided to cover the mine with brush and tree branches to make it appear as part of the landscape. He also covered the gold cache carefully so that no one would suspect anything was hidden there. Then he loaded his burros with his personal belongings and mining paraphernalia and started out for Copper City. Along the way he tried to make up a story about his partner and how he came to be leaving the claim. He bruised himself and cut off one ear to make it appear that Indians had attacked them at camp and killed Dupont.

Thompson didn't tarry long at Copper City; his conscience would not let him stay close to the place where his life had been so suddenly uprooted. Wanting to get away from the country as far as possible, he sold his burros and went back home to Texas. There he told an elaborate story of how the Indians had come upon him and Dupont one evening, killed his partner, and in the struggle had succeeded in cutting off one of his own ears before he could escape. The only detail he omitted was the mine and the wealth he had left buried in a scrub oak clump. He planned to go back and retrieve the gold coins, but he had to wait until time had erased the memory of that fatal Sunday morning.

Time eventually helped Thompson to forget the events that had led to his coming back to Texas, and he had told the story of the Indian attack so many times that he had begun to believe that it had actually taken place. The only thing that he could not forget as time went on was the mine and the wealth that was back on the Gallina Mountains near Cuba, New Mexico. As times got harder and employment became scarce for a man who was a prospector and miner rather than a cowhand or farmer, he began to think more definitely about returning. Eventually he found himself constantly thinking about Copper City and old Mathias and his store, and step by step taking himself mentally to the place where he had been happy mining gold.

One day in the spring of 1900 he decided to go back to the mountains of New Mexico. He waited only for the weather to warm up enough to make travel more comfortable in the high country; then he set out west and kept going until he reached the village of Cuba. Here he stayed for a few days trying to find out what he could about the mine in the Gallina Mountains. But people had ceased to talk about Indian attacks and killings that had taken place so long before; they had other things to talk about. In the little cantina where miners and prospectors came down to slake their thirst, he finally found an old-timer who remembered something about the death of Harris Dupont.

"Yeah," he said, "that was some time ago, but they found the fellow who done it. He had his gold watch with him; that's how they come to find him."

Thompson had been away in Texas and had never heard about this development. He pressed his newly found acquaintance for more details:

"Where is this fellow? You remember his name?"

The old prospector took another deep swallow of whiskey and answered:

"Yeah, I recollect now who he was. The paper said his name was Perfecto Padilla, a sheepherder who was in that part of the country when Harris Dupont was murdered. They hanged him for it up in Santa Fe, but they never found Dupont's partner's body."

Thompson asked no more questions. This information brought up another name to add to his conscience and helped to revive the memory of the man he had almost come to believe the Indians had killed. Needing something strong to settle his stomach, he called the bartender and ordered another bottle.

A few days later Thompson set out for the mine. For a while he was on familiar ground, but as he walked into the mountains things began to change. Some of the new roads broke up the landmarks he was accustomed to. The rains, the wind, and the winter snows had erased the place where the partners had once washed their ore, and the mountain slopes had lost their familiarity. He looked for an opening covered with brush and trees where years before he and Dupont had mined successfully for gold, but all he found in the vicinity was a goat corral. One morning he met a grizzled old mountaineer who owned some of the goats and talked to him about a mining camp, but the old man knew nothing about it.

"Quién sabe," he said; "maybe sometime ago somebody look for gold. I don't know him. What was his name?"

Thompson mentioned Harris Dupont's name and the old timer remembered:

"Oh yes, señor, many years ago he was killed by a sheep-herder but I never knew him."

This information reminded Thompson that someone else had paid a debt for him, and the thought took his mind from gold and mining. He thanked the old-timer and walked back to Cuba. From there he rode across to Albuquerque with the memory now an obsession. He had to tell someone that Perfecto Padilla hadn't killed Dupont, that *he* had pounded his partner's head with a sledge hammer in a fit of anger. And yet he had no desire to turn himself in. He turned this over in his mind as he rode into Albuquerque through the old town. The bells of the old church of San Felipe were ringing in the plaza as he hitched his horse in front of the cantina and went in for a drink. The deep tolling of the bells continued as he drank at the bar, and from them he got an idea that would solve his problem.

That night he sat up most of the night in the *fonda* where he had taken a room, and wrote an exact account of what had happened back in the eighties in the Gallina Mountains. He wrote it down as a confession and began it: "In the name of our Lord I want to make this true confession . . ." He was not a Catholic but the thought prevailed in his mind that if he told any clergyman what he had done his guilt would dissipate.

Early the next day Thompson started north to Santa Fe. He wanted to inquire about the man who had been hanged at the state penitentiary and in some way attempt to clear his name without implicating himself. As he was approaching the village of Alameda north of Albuquerque he saw a priest coming out of the church. This was a bit of luck he hadn't expected. Unceremoniously he handed him the confession he had written out the night before, and continued on his way to Santa Fe to clear Perfecto Padilla, the innocent man who had probably found the body of Dupont and stolen the watch still on him. The priest took the envelope, paused for a moment, and then put it into his side pocket. But Thompson did not look back; he was on his way to Santa Fe to try to do a good deed. . . .

Many years later a young man named Andres Carbajal was hunting turkeys in the Gallina Mountains and accidentally came across a partly covered cave. He cleared enough of the entrance to go in and soon found himself in a long tunnel running straight into the mountain. He was not a miner, but there was enough evidence to show him that this had been a working claim. His father was away at a ranch when he found the mine, and he had to return to Colorado, where he was employed; and so he sent the senior Carbajal a description of the location, hoping the older man would investigate it. Then, to make sure that his father comprehended the directions, he added:

> In order to understand my description better, go in the direction of San Pedro hill, which you know better than I, . . . But first try to locate the spring. This is almost erased at the bottom of the canyon. You'll find there the place where they used to wash the ore . . . the vats, pans and some posts. The mine is just behind this on the side where the sun sets . . .

Apparently the elder Carbajal was not too well acquainted with the country around the Gallina Mountains, to judge by a post script that Andres added in the same letter:

> Julian Montano and Joaquin Casados (the first one from San Antonio) are sheepherders who live in Cuba and know the Gallina Mountains very well.

San Pedro Hill, referred to by Andres Carbajal, is more than a hill; it is a mountain peak close to eleven thousand feet high in the middle of the rugged Jemez Mountains of north central New Mexico. Anyone going "in the direction of San Pedro Hill," as the letter to Andres' father directed, would have to know in what direction; otherwise he would have to cover a distance of twenty miles from east to west and three times that from north to south.

The mine was never found, and Andres remained in Colorado after the death of his father. The last letter directed to him returned from Mancos, Colorado, with a stamped message reading: ADDRESS UNKNOWN.

CHAPTER 11

NATURAL PHENOMENA AND THE GROWTH OF LEGENDS

◆

LEGENDS ARE AN INTERESTING PRODUCT of folk society, the origin of which dates back to pre-Christian days, to Greece, Babylon, and the valley of the Nile. They are so deeply imbedded in the cultural texture of the folk, so inextricably woven into the pattern of folk thinking that today, as in the days of the Greeks, even geological formations assume anthropomorphic shapes and are indued with the attributes of folk heroes. It is through this thought process that a jutting peak, a profile on a canyon wall, or a depression in a rock becomes a giant, an angel, or a kneeling nun.

Ordinarily, a legend may begin with an actual happening or with something that tradition accepts as fact. A simple story may be gradually embellished with whatever attributes are important to the folk, and with whatever concepts are current and acceptable at the time when it begins. These cultural attributes cannot be judged by standards of a cultivated society. Even the element of time cannot be measured by the calendar, for historicity and scientific truth are not standards of folk thinking. Moreover, in order to determine what is wise or foolish, kind or cruel, beautiful or ugly, the folk resort indiscriminately to supernatural revelation, transformation, and coincidence. Once the legend is formed and widely disseminated, the factual assumes a secondary role. It is folly to try to verify some legends. It is like trying to determine whether the carriage in which Cinderella rode to the ball was actually made from a pumpkin. All one can do is adduce from the facts surrounding a legend how the story might have started in the first place.

Very often the actual fact or historical account that gives rise to a particular legend may be totally forgotten, lost, or modified to such an extent that only the legend growing from the original happening survives. Folk audiences, or *la gente* as they are called in Spanish, do not question historical accuracy, mainly because they are not concerned with it. A legend need only be interesting and plausible, that is, plausible in that it conforms to folk values. Unlike the fairy tale, where characters, events, and places are representative types such as kings, dragons, and giants, the legend usually is credible enough to show that the initial event or personage could have happened or could have existed, even though the events are ascribed to some inanimate geological formation. No factual evidence may be advanced to prove that a pirate buried his loot on a given island, or that the pirate actually existed, for that matter, but he *could have* and, therefore, *might have,* easily existed and cached away chests filled with gold. The conjecture arising from this possibility is converted into the sort of legend that circulates as fact among those whose imagination has not been dulled by disuse.

In the southwestern United States where overpopulation has not completely destroyed the old landmarks, there are many legends still associated with geographical locations. Such names as Las Animas, Starvation Peak, Enchanted Mesa, the Kneeling Nun and Hermit's Peak are but a few of these landmarks, of which the names originated long ago. There are likewise many names of men and women, whose familiarity to us today has been enhanced by the legends that surround them. Were we to divest "Judge" Roy Bean, Billy the Kid, and a host of other well-known characters of the legendary aura that has given them stature and popularity, they would sink into relative anonymity and perhaps never would have become so famous or infamous. This aural fiction, so to speak, is the prelude to the literature that has been written about people, places, and events in the Southwest. Despite jet-propelled aircraft, intercontinental missiles, and atomic explosions, there are a few places left in the mountains of New Mexico and Colorado and in the plains of Texas where old-timers can lean against an adobe wall on sunny winter days or sit under an *alamo* in the summer time to tell their *compadres* about buried treasures, haunted canyons, Indian raids, and strange men like the Hermit of Las Vegas or the romantic nun who perished through her worldly indecision.

In the copper mining country of southern New Mexico, near the city of Santa Rita, there stands a prominence on the Pinos Altos mountain range to which tradition has given the name of "The Kneeling Nun." The story ascribed to this physical feature has been told in prose and poetry for many years, and has become so much a part of the surrounding countryside that when the New Mexico Highway Department planned to blast away the crumbling rock for safety reasons, the people around Santa Rita circulated a petition and had the rock reinforced with concrete in order to preserve the legendary site.

Some writers have considered the story of the nun a misleading fabrication, its origin spurious, and the existence of the mission nun a mere "myth." Aside from the ethical or moral antecedents of the nun's questionable existence, the fact is that there is something truly mythical about the legend that has grown up around her. Like the myths of classical Greece, the story of the Kneeling Nun is concerned with a dweller in a god-like orbit whose passions made her descend to an earthly atmosphere and participate in the amorous delights of tragedy-ridden mortals. And like the Greek mythical characters, the nun has been transformed into a geophysical formation, where she continues her legendary existence. We may not accept the legend as being based on fact, but the story of the romantic, repentant nun of Santa Rita is still told, and the prominence on the mountain top still stands as a monument to what the folk like to imagine might have, or could have, happened in Spanish colonial days long ago.

According to the legend, there was a Spanish mission in the vicinity of what is now Santa Rita, where the Indians were taught the Spanish language and their children were instructed in the ways of the Catholic Church. Among the inmates of this far-flung outpost there was a young and attractive nun, whose unselfish ways and patient ministering to the Indians had won their friendship and admiration. Life was simple and even monotonous at times, except for those who like the young nun had dedicated themselves to serve in a land that was far from prodigal.

During the hot summer days, the nuns found respite from their labors sitting in the shade of the fruit trees in the high-walled patio surrounding the mission. Late one afternoon, while they were enjoying a short rest in the garden, one of the Indian servants came running to tell them that a soldier was at the gates asking to be admitted.

"He is very sick and wants water," the Indian added.

As strangers were always welcome at the mission, the servant was told to bring the soldier in. To the nuns' surprise two Indians returned holding up and almost dragging between them a man in a tattered, dust-covered uniform, scuffed boots, and no hat. His badly sunburned face, his bloodshot eyes, and swollen lips gave him the appearance of a man cast upon the desert to die. He was, in fact, almost dead. When the nuns tried to speak to him, his head rolled limply from side to side and he uttered a hoarse grunt.

The soldier was taken inside, where the nuns bathed his

bleeding lips and gave him water with a spoon until he had absorbed enough liquid to ease his thirst; but he was completely overcome by the heat of the desert, over which he had wandered aimlessly for several days after losing his way in a blinding sandstorm. For many days he lingered at the mission, a victim of exposure, dehydration, and sunstroke.

The young nun took care of the soldier as he lay in a coma in one of the cell-like rooms. She bathed his burning face during the day and sat by his bedside late into the night waiting for some sign of his recovery. Her patience was finally rewarded, when he stirred and gradually regained consciousness. He became aware of a blurred, white form moving near him; everything around him looked white. He closed his eyes and sketchily began to recall the nightmare of the desert—the wind-driven sand, the search for his lost horse, the beating sun, and his thirst. He remembered vaguely the outline of the mission, like another tantalizing vision that would vanish into the hot atmosphere before he could reach it. He had been deceived so many times by mirages of lakes and cities that he had never expected to reach the cluster of buildings and trees surrounded by spectral mountains; but he had dragged himself toward the alluring phantasm hoping it would materialize.

Now in the reveries of his feverish mind he thought he had awakened in heaven. A pang of conscience reminded him for a moment that his life on earth had not been exemplary. When the fever finally abated, he opened his eyes and realized that he was still alive, very weak, and very tired. Where was he? His body felt as though it had been crushed and beaten, and his throat still felt dry. He looked around the strange place where he lay and noticed the whitewashed walls, the door, and the high window, through the wooden shutters of which he could hear the trees rustling in the breeze. Just then the door opened gently, and a young nun tiptoed toward his bed. This was the blurred vision he had seen earlier in the day. His first effort to speak produced an unpleasant rasping sound, and before he could clear his throat to speak again, she raised a finger to her mouth and shook her head. Once more she placed a moist cloth on his forehead, felt his pulse, and smiling disappeared through the door.

Others came later to attend to him; he looked into their faces trying to find the features of the nun he had seen before. At dinner time she returned with the boy who brought his tray and remained long enough for him to tell his story. From her he learned the details of his arrival at the mission gate. In the weeks that followed, the young nun and the recovering soldier came to know each other intimately. Their friendship grew into such a close personal attachment that both began to dread the day when he would rejoin his regiment. One day as he was walking in the garden alone, he met her accidentally; thereafter their meetings were deliberately planned.

Finally a messenger arrived with a new mount for the now fully-recovered soldier, with orders also for him to report to the garrison where he was assigned. He purposely drew out for several days his preparations to leave, pleading his case all the while and trying to persuade the nun to go with him. When it became apparent that he had lost his suit, he saddled his horse and rode away from the mission. No sooner had he left, than the nun, abandoning her original resolve, resigned herself to the inevitable consequences and walked past the gates hoping to overtake her lover. She followed his trail, but he was already beyond reach.

The day had run its course, she had failed to join her lover, and she knew the doors of the mission were closed behind her. As she approached one of the peaks of the Pinos Altos Range, she decided to climb to the top and scan the plains below for the traveler who was riding farther and farther away from her. By dusk she reached the summit and knelt down to look over the horizon, but she failed to get a glimpse of her soldier lover.

She remained kneeling, a sorrowing, repentant mortal cast out from the orbit of her former usefulness, high on a mountain top, alone. When the sun rose the following morning, she was still there looking over the plains, and she is still there today, a permanent monument to a love that did not prosper but that served to christen a mountain prominence in the Pinos Altos Range, "The Kneeling Nun."

Another natural phenomenon forming the source from which legends grow may be seen in the fireballs of the Sandias. Old-timers who live in the Río Grande Valley near Albuquerque often speak of the lights they have seen floating down from these mountains east of the city and disappearing over the extinct volcanoes west of the river. A motorist claims that while driving down from the mountains on the scenic Rim Road, he was almost forced off the highway by bright lights, which at first seemed to be the headlights of an approaching car. As he came to a sharp curve, the lights suddenly swerved upon him, bounced back upon the canyon wall, and went out as though someone had turned them off. He stopped the car, got out, and looked around, but he could not see a trace nor hear the sound of another car.

A man by the name of Ben Baca living in Martinez Town, as North Arno Street was known when it was a suburb of Albuquerque, had been hunting over the mesas toward the Sandia Mountains and was returning home after dark. As he walked down an arroyo, he noticed a firelight down the slope about a half-mile below and assumed that sheepherders were making camp for the night. As it was still early, he decided to stop by and talk with them; sheepherders always interested him. He had walked quite a distance when he discovered that he was not getting any closer to the camp; the light seemed just as far as when he had first sighted it. Strange thought he, how deceptive distances can be at night.

After awhile Mr. Baca began to see the lights of Martinez Town, and also realized that there was no sheep camp but only a ball of fire about the size of a large pumpkin rolling along in the direction he was moving. Instinctively he raised his gun and fired, and simultaneously the ball bounded into the air. It must be a witch! he thought. With his knife he cut a cross on the nose of his next bullet and fired again. The ball of fire bounced out of range every time he shot at it. Ben stood still for a moment trying to decide whether to run the rest of the way home or shout for help. To his relief, he heard a familiar voice calling him: *"Compadre, compadre!"* Nothing could have been more welcome than the company of a friend at a time like this.

"Yes, *compadre,* where are you? Did you see that apparition? I thought I was going to be bewitched!"

To his surprise, there was no answer, no footsteps of the friend he thought was coming to join him, simply the ball of fire quietly resting, waiting for him to shoot again. Instead of continuing down the arroyo into town, Ben Baca turned sharply south hoping the ball would not accompany him so close to town, but the thing bounded out of the arroyo and continued to roll ahead of him. Once more the familiar voice spoke:

"Don't be alarmed, *compadre.* Just promise me to have a Mass said for the repose of my soul."

Ben Baca was willing to promise anything that would rid him of the fireball, but despite his fear he was able to recognize that it was the voice of a friend long since dead. He promised to carry out the request, and the light vanished over the cemetery on the edge of town, much to the relief of a very frightened Mr. Baca.

For many years, fireballs have been reported over the mountains from Santa Fe to Albuquerque, a recent published account appearing in the Santa Fe *New Mexican* of December 5, 1949:

156

Fireball Seen by Residents over Santa Fe

Two reports to Santa Fe police and one to the *New Mexican* testified to the appearance of a 'fireball' in the sky over this area last evening.

At 8:58 P.M., Howard Atkins, King's Rest Court, Cerrillos Road, called the police to say that he had seen a large ball of fire heading down towards the mountains near Bishop's Lodge.

Bill Elwell, East Palace, and Kieth Ryan, Cerro Gordo, were visiting H. L. Wilbourn at his ranch in Rinconada, and while the three were waiting for a bus at 7:45 saw a ball of fire in the northeastern sky . . .

I was terrified when I first saw these fireballs as a young boy back in 1917. A friend from El Paso by the name of Frank García and I were walking south one evening on what is now Highway 85 on our way to a basketball game at Menaul School. In those days the road was an unpaved trail through *salitre* marshes bordered by tall tamerisks. The two of us walked along talking as young boys usually do, trying to keep warm on a cold November night. We were about half a mile from Menaul Road on what is now North Fourth Street, when we noticed two yellow lights halfway up the mountainside to the east of the highway. Frank saw them first and pointed them out:

"Look, there must be some sheepherders camping for the night over yonder."

I looked up and saw what appeared to be two campfires fairly close together, and wondered if it was as cold in the mountains as it was down in the valley where we were.

We continued along the dark highway and soon forgot what we had seen; getting to the gymnasium to see a basketball game was much more important. We left the road about a mile below where we had noticed the campfires and turned east toward the Sandias. In the moonless night the two lights suddenly came into view, but this time they had moved to the base of the mountains. It seemed strange that they should have shifted so visibly, but on second thought Frank and I decided that the angle from which we were now looking at them accounted for the apparent change in position. Presently we came to a rise on the road as we approached the railroad crossing, and from this vantage point discovered that the lights were moving slowly to the west. This finally solved the riddle, so we thought for a moment. Mountaineer woodhaulers in those days used to drive down Bear Canyon at night with a lantern hanging on the left side of their wagons, and we had first taken these lantern lights for campfires as they drove down the mountainside.

We had just arrived at this logical explanation as we reached the Santa Fe railroad tracks, and then the lights rose about fifty feet into the air. Woodhaulers didn't fly, and back in 1917 there were no airplanes flying at night. Had it happened today, anyone would have sworn they were flying saucers. Frank had just begun to tell me that the lights were railroad signal lights, but he stopped short when the balls of fire crossed the tracks and rose above the ground. Simultaneously they began moving toward the two most frightened little boys in the state of New Mexico. I wanted to run, but my legs didn't respond; my hand kept reaching out trying to touch Frank, but he had suddenly vanished. For what must have been a few seconds, my eyes never left the lights. I was hoping they would change their course, and to my great relief they began moving west toward the Río Grande. I looked around on the ground and finally made out the outline of my companion who had fallen on his knees and was earnestly appealing to the saints for deliverance from the apparition.

The lights, as I recall, were about the size and brightness of a harvest moon, always moving about twenty feet apart and at about twice a man's walking gait. Our fright being temporarily over, we watched the fireballs until they disappeared beyond the river toward the extinct volcanoes on the west. Then we went on to the basketball game. On the way back, we joined some of the older boys just to be sure we had stronger company. They didn't believe our story, of course; and pooh-poohed at us, saying that we were scared of the dark and were seeing things.

I never saw these lights again, although I often heard others talk about them, until the fall of 1930. This time there was only one light, but the place was about the same as that where Frank and I had seen them thirteen years before. On my way back from Denver, I stopped to get some gas at a filling station on North Albuquerque Street. I've forgotten the name of the man who ran the service station, but we were looking in the direction of the nearby Sandia Mountains, where the full moon could be seen just over the rim.

"Moon's out awful late tonight," he remarked.

I agreed with him and paid no more attention to it; bright moons are no novelty in the dry atmosphere of the Southwest. As I was paying for the gas, however, I was surprised to see the "moon" halfway down the mountain instead of in the sky where normal moons usually stay, and called it to the attention of the service station man.

"Well, I'll be damned! You know, that's the second time that bright light has fooled me since I've been running this station. I always think it's the moon."

He and I discussed every possibility that would explain this appearance, but as it was with Frank and me years before, we couldn't come up with anything plausible. The service man said with finality:

"I'll betcha that's nothing but a witch from that mountain village of San Antonio. They've got plenty of 'em up there."

I've been curious about those lights since the first time I saw them, but no one has been able to explain them. When I was on the faculty of the University of New Mexico at Albuquerque, I mentioned the phenomenon to Dr. Jack Workman, Chairman of the Physics Department, and I agreed to call him any time I saw them no matter what time of night it was. He was working on a meteorological project and had rigged up some instruments in a truck that could go almost anywhere when necessary. Unfortunately I never saw the lights again, and as World War II came along at about that time Jack and I never had a chance to look into the matter scientifically. He went on with some highly classified defense work and made a name for himself. Meanwhile, the lights, according to the press, still float over the mesas by the Sandia Mountains and leave people to conjecture about witches on a broomstick, and more recently about flying saucers.

CHAPTER 12

THE HERMIT OF LAS VEGAS

◆

THE NEW MEXICO Highway Department has a sign on Highway 85 near Las Vegas pointing to a mountain to the west of the road called "Hermit's Peak." The legend on this sign briefly states the origin of the name and gives a few facts regarding a hermit who lived there about the time of the Civil War. The story behind the sign tells about a man born in Italy in 1800 who traveled over three continents during his long, arduous, and eventful life before coming to New Mexico, where he spent the last seven years of his restless wanderings. Almost a century has elapsed since he walked into Las Vegas alongside of a Santa Fe Trail wagon train, but the mountaineers speak of him as though he were a contemporary still living among them.

Wherever he went, this old anchorite sought a secluded cave on some nearby mountain and stayed in it until the urge to travel sent him in search of another cave in a distant land. The oral and written accounts he gave of his life before he was found murdered on the slopes of the Organ Mountains in southern New Mexico mention Spain, Canada, and most of the countries in Latin America. One of the factors that has helped to keep the Hermit's name alive is this lofty, double-headed peak named for him by Rodney B. Schoonmacher, a New Mexican pioneer. The mountain, eighteen miles west of Las Vegas, had been

known to local folk as "Cerro del Tecolote," and to many others by the prosaic designation of "Baldy" until Mr. Schoonmacher gave it the name that linked it to the legend.

The first authentic account of the Hermit of Las Vegas was written by Schoonmacher in 1939.[1] He gave the anchorite's name as Giovanni Maria Agustine. In subsequent stories, many of them unreliable, it has gone through such variations as Marie Agustine, Juan Bautista Agustiniani, Matteo Boccalini, Father Francesco, "el Solitario," and Juan Maria Agostini. It has never been strictly determined what his actual name was, but the name by which he is traditionally known today is simply "el Ermitaño" in Spanish, and "the Hermit" in English. According to the records that he is supposed to have had with him when he was killed, he was born in Italy, the son of a noble or distinguished family. Writers do not agree as to his birthplace. Some say that he was a native of Capri; even Sardinia is mentioned. Equally conflicting are the accounts of his death. Authors who have relied on oral statements gathered from secondary sources have him dying at the hands of the Indians in Socorro, New Mexico, or murdered, stabbed, filled with arrows, and even tortured by treasure-seekers who thought he had quantities of gold in his possession.

How the Hermit came to leave his home and go wandering over the world is also a conjectural subject. Some say that he

---

[1] "Missionary Gave Name to Hermit's Peak," *Las Vegas Daily Optic,* June 3, 1939, 3–4.

Some writers have mentioned that Mr. Schoonmaker became acquainted with the Hermit while employed by the Ilfeld Company as a bookkeeper; but if we are to go by his own statement, this is not possible. He prefaced his account:

"Fifty-five years ago, upon arrival in Las Vegas, this writer made the acquaintance of several persons who had been friends of the stranger, and from them were gathered the reminiscences set down here."

This was written by Mr. Schoonmaker in 1939. That would place his arrival in Las Vegas in 1884, or fifteen years after the Hermit's death. However, Schoonmaker had access to informants whose recollection of the recluse must have been still vivid.

renounced the gayety and splendorous living in which his father sought to rear him. Others insist that in penance for his misdeeds he left the comforts of home and decided upon a life of total abstinence. The most romantic account of his life of solitude tells us that while studying for the priesthood he fell in love with a "bewitching dark-eyed and lustrous-haired beauty, and the succeptible young priest, alas, succumbed to the wiles of the radiant maiden, and he fell in a most earthly way!" This same imaginative writer informs us that the Hermit took orders at the age of twenty-one, and that he eventually became secretary to the pope.

The source from which the details of his private life stem today seems to be an elusive folder or "binder" that he had with him at the time of his death. Schoonmacher, in the article previously mentioned, said:

> In this book or binder is a series of passports and letters of introduction from a score or more of different countries by numerous government and city officials. These are in several languages. From this book we learn that the name of the wanderer was Giovanni Maria Agustine, an Italian whose journeying began in the year of 1827, that being the earliest date found in these papers.

Charles Wolfe,[2] another native Las Vegan, is supposed to have had access likewise to the original papers of the Hermit for the preparation of a manuscript in four parts which he apparently never finished before he died. In part I he states:

> The history of the "Wonder of Our Century," as he was called in 1846 by the *Mercurio Volante of Valparaiso*, will be told in the following record, according to the authentic papers of the "Wandering Solitary" as his title should have been. These papers

[2] According to his family Charles Wolfe copied the original papers of the Hermit and left the manuscript with the Brothers at Saint Michael's College in Santa Fe. Brother James of the College made Mr. Wolfe's copy available to me.

have been thoroughly examined and classified by the author of this story. They contain in a reduced form the whole life of the pious man as dictated by himself in defense of his honor when attacked by persecutors, or in excuse of his refusal of the Holy Orders, when ordered to receive them by several Bishops, his friends and admirers. The work of the writer has been limited to arranging and translating these documents. This little work is divided into four chapters corresponding to the principal places visited by the Hermit.

In the body of the paper, Mr. Wolfe tells us that the Hermit's name was Juan de Agostini, and that he was born in the Province of Novara in Lombardy. There is no Province of Novara, but there is a small village by that name in Piedmont, which is next to Lombardy. The Hermit's mother, who died when the boy was only eight months old, was Donimica Norrina de Funtanetto, and his father was a nobleman named Mattias Agostini.

The Hermit's book, portfolio, or binder, as it is referred to by various writers, has had a long and fateful history since it first came into the possession of Colonel Albert J. Fountain of Mesilla, New Mexico, when the owner was found dead in 1896. The Colonel was a close friend of a trader from Las Vegas named Manuel Romero, who had been the Hermit's principal benefactor and friend since their meeting in Council Grove, Kansas, during Civil War days.

After the Hermit's death, Mr. Romero asked Colonel Fountain for the binder containing the Hermit's autobiography, and thereafter the papers remained in the Romero family, passing to his son Margarito Romero and thence to Hipólito Baca, a retired United States marshal living in Santa Fe. But apparently certain items of this collection of documents were not contained in the binder given to Manuel Romero: Mrs. Teresita García de Fountain, a ninety-three-year-old daughter-in-law of Colonel Fountain, informed me in 1952 that some of the papers had been loaned to Father Kupper in Embudo Canyon, on the road to Taos.[3] I called on Father Kupper that same year and looked through the chronicle the Hermit had kept in several languages, including a very poor version of Latin.

Having learned that Señor Hipólito Baca, grandson of the original Romero, had the binder with the most important papers, I drove down from Denver to see him and have a look at the Hermit's own story. Mr. Baca, a charming Spanish old gentleman, now totally blind, received me with enthusiasm, glad to talk to someone interested in the events of his youth. He had such a clear and resonant voice that I asked permission to record the interview on wire. (This was before the advent of tape recorders.) Despite the fact that I had read everything I could find written for the past century about the Hermit, I felt that a direct descendant from the man who had befriended him and brought him to New Mexico could give me additional details not to be found elsewhere. For one thing, Mr. Baca had been born just a few years after the death of the recluse and might have heard something still untold. As the logical thing was to begin at the beginning, I asked him when he first heard about the old man.

I first heard about the Hermit about sixty-five years ago or more, when I was just a young boy and was living with my uncle, Don Margarito Romero, at El Porvenir which is right at the foot of Hermit's Peak. We used to go up to the Peak on sight-seeing expeditions because from the top you can see over two hundred miles around. Many people from the surrounding villages of Rosiada, Manuelitas, and Sapello formed a Society called 'La Sociedad del Ermitaño,' and they went up there twice a year in May and in September. They put up a lot of crosses, a sort of Way of the Cross or *Via Crucis*.

Some of the people say that these crosses were put up by the

---

[3] Both Mrs. Fountain and Father Kupper have died since my visit.

Penitentes, as you have probably heard, but it has no connection with it. These people didn't do any penance whatever. They began the procession at a place where the Hermit had built his cabin on top. The Hermit didn't actually build this cabin but the people who felt sorry for him did it, and they put it right over the spring so he wouldn't have to go out for water. The door to his cabin was about two feet long and just tall enough for him to crawl through it. They put some nails all along the edges just to keep the wild animals out, at least that's what I had always been told. I don't know what sort of roof they put on it because when I saw the cabin the roof had already caved in, but I suppose it was a roof like they use in that part of the country.

Down about three hundred feet on the south side of the Peak, there is a big cave where another log cabin was built over another spring. This cave is hard to get at unless you know the trail to it.

When I asked Mr. Baca about the Society formed by the people of the surrounding villages, he answered:

This Society was formed to keep up the good work which the Hermit had done. He used to come down to the villages and read religious books and talk to the people. He was not a priest, but when he was approaching one of the villages, my uncle used to tell me that the children ran into their houses so they wouldn't have to kneel and say prayers. They could always tell he was coming by the sound of the little bell attached to his walking staff.

Mr. Baca gave me the history of how the Hermit taught children to read when he went to Las Vegas during the summer months, and how he would refuse lodging in people's homes, preferring to sleep in the open and cook his own corn meal mush, the only food he was known to eat in New Mexico. Throughout the interview, the old United States marshal refuted the many stories of the miracles the Hermit had performed. He shook his head and raised his hand saying:

167

No, no, there's nothing to that at all. He couldn't perform miracles. He didn't believe in the teachings of the Catholic Church and specially the sacraments. He was a religious man, a good man interested in being good to people, but not a miracle man.

One of the many stories about the Hermit's death says that he was persecuted by the Church because of the influence he had among the folk, and also because he did not subscribe to its teachings. One of these stories goes so far as to mention the name of a certain priest living in Deming, New Mexico, who supposedly heard the confession of the man who killed the Hermit in the Organ Mountains in the spring of 1869. Mr. Baca was of the opinion that he had been killed by the Indians, possibly the Apaches, who were on the warpath so often during the past century. There was some correspondence contained in the portfolio I was seeking that told of the Hermit's death, and at the conclusion of the interview I asked Mr. Baca for the privilege of looking over the papers, which had been in his family for three generations.

"You are certainly welcome to see them," he answered, "but I don't have them in the house. I loaned them, or rather, put them up as security with one of my former associates when I had to make a loan. Miss Belles, who lives not far from here, has them. I'm sure she'll be glad to let you have the entire portfolio. Just tell her that I sent you over, or she can call me on the phone to verify it."

I was glad to hear that Miss Belles also lived in Santa Fe, where I could contact her. The lady was very surprised, however, to learn that Mr. Baca had forgotten that she had returned the Hermit's papers many years before.

"Why it must have been about ten years ago that I returned the papers to Mr. Baca when we were both working in the Federal Building. He probably has forgotten he has them."

I was beginning to realize how a treasure-hunter must feel when he is about to put his hands on the "other half of the treasure map" and finds that it is just one step ahead of him. I returned to Mr. Baca's home and told him what Miss Belles had said. It was his turn to be surprised:

"Now, isn't that strange! She probably doesn't remember. I'm sure she has them yet. Why don't you take me up to see her? I should like to say hello to my friend anyhow."

We drove up to Miss Belles' house and called on her. She was very happy to see her former associate and friend, and together they went over the details about the papers. Both were equally sure of their contentions and tried to conjecture what might have happened to the binder. I listened attentively for any word that might give me a clue to the whereabouts of the now missing papers, but no mustering of Sherlock Holmes savvy helped to shed any light upon their disappearance. The ultimate source on the Hermit's life was apparently lost or misplaced. The vexing thing about it was that although many writers have claimed to have read the anchorite's own story from this binder, no two written accounts seem to agree even on some of the basic details. As late as 1955 the *Albuquerque Tribune* quoted the story of a *Chicago Tribune* correspondent who "paused in Las Vegas in 1882 to gather stories and legends about Hermit Peak, a mountain northwest of the town."[4]

This story is even wilder than most. The correspondent described the Hermit as a Spaniard about thirty years of age, who had come to the Peak in 1835, and met his death because of rumors that he had collected a fortune in gold. The murderers had appeared to him in a dream, and so he went out into the plains to meet them early one morning and was killed.

In all probability, Juan Maria Agostini started on his pil-

[4] Howard Bryan, "Hermit Peak Legend," *Albuquerque Tribune,* November 24, 1955.

grimage when he was about thirty years of age. He first went to Spain, arriving at the shrine of Santiago de Compostela in Galicia on February 27, 1831. When I visited Compostela in the winter of 1953, I tried to find some records that might mention the visit of this Italian, who was later to become the West's most famous Hermit; but because at Compostela pilgrims have not been a novelty for the past thousand years, one more devotee among the multitudes coming over the *Camino de Francia* apparently had not made much of an impression upon the Galician Spaniards.

From Compostela in northwestern Spain, the Hermit traveled east to the shrine of Nuestra Señora del Pilar in the old Roman city of Zaragoza, and continued to the Catalonian sanctuary of Monserrat near Barcelona. For five years, according to his account, he went about from shrine to shrine and sanctuary to sanctuary in search of peace and seclusion. He tried to become a Cartusian and then a Trappist monk, but neither of these orders seemed to satisfy his craving for a life of absolute solitude. While in this state of inner conflict and indecision, the Virgin is supposed to have appeared to him beckoning westward with her outstretched arm. Following her entreaty, he crossed the Atlantic and came to Caracas in 1838. According to Mr. Wolfe, this is a faithful translation of the Hermit's chronicle:

> When I arrived in Caracas, the capital of the newly formed Republic of Venezuela, a new life began for me. In fact, I knew nothing of South America, except that it had high mountains and extensive deserts. This was what I was looking for in order to enter fully into a life of perfect solitude.
>
> After a few days of rest in this city, I continued my travels going through Santa Fe de Bogotá, Papayan [Popayán], Quito, Guayaquil, Lambayeque, and Motupe. I lived in these different places for a variable time, and preached to the people according to the order I received from the Bishops.

In Caracas, Bogotá, and Lambayeque, the Bishops wanted to raise me to the priesthood and retain me in the Diocese, but when I explained to them the vow I had taken and the vocation I had received, they allowed me to proceed.

In Motupe, province of Lambayeque [in northern Peru], I spent two years in a cave on the side of a high spur of the Andes. My dwelling was twelve miles distant from the village, but this did not prevent me from going to the parish church every Sunday and feast day to assist at Mass. I was young then, and walking was a real pleasure.

When I was in Spain, I visited all the places mentioned by the Hermit in his chronicle, and then picked up his trail in South America in the village of Motupe. The alcalde of the village had never heard of a hermit in that vicinity, and since the Hermit's account did not state the direction of the cave it would have been necessary to explore the mountains for a radius of twelve miles in order to locate his "dwelling." Another reason why not even the oldest residents had ever heard of a hermit in their vicinity is that the life led by most of the people in the mountains of Peru is almost hermitic. The presence of one more troglodyte like Juan Maria Agostini was no novelty.

From Motupe the Hermit went south along the coast of Peru and visited Trujillo, a coastal city founded by the conquistador, Pizarro. He did not tarry long but went up to a village that today has become famous for its newly developed mining industry known as "Cerro de Pasco Mining Corporation."

I reached Cerro de Pasco where I spent several months at an altitude of 12,000 feet above sea level. On November 4, 1842 I was in the capital of Peru, Lima. Here again the Archbishop insisted on my becoming a priest, but I could not consent; my vocation called me to solitude, not to the exalted ministry of the priesthood.

He retraced his steps from Lima in April of 1843, and on

May 6 of the same year reached the Marañon River to the northeast, one of the large tributaries to the Amazon in Peru. He actually entered the Amazon at Tabatinga, a little village where
Brazil, Peru, and Ecuador come together. Although he does not
say so, the Hermit probably took a boat down the Amazon; he
could not have made the journey on foot through the jungle.
He covers the length of the river with a simple statement:

> I continued eastward and reached the mouth of the mighty
> river, then, following the coast, passed through Bahia, Pernam-
> buco, and stopped some time in Rio Janeiro.

The *Bahia* mentioned by him is the present city of Salvador,
halfway between the mouth of the Amazon and Rio de Janeiro.
Pernambuco is the name by which Recife was known in the
nineteenth century. In all probability the Hermit either dictated
this account to someone or wrote it from memory many years
after he made the trip; for the order in which he would have
traveled should have been first Recife and then Salvador.

Those who have read the contents of the lost binder say
that it contained a number of letters of recommendation given
the Hermit by governors and men in high places. Mr. Wolfe,
quoting the chronicle of the Hermit in reference to his visit to
Brazil says:

> The Emperor Pedro II took me into his friendship and show-
> ered me with kindnesses and favors as he could not have done
> for any other person. These honors, however, were not to my
> taste for solitude and hardship, therefore I left the Brazilian
> capital never to return.

By his own admission he must have been born in 1801 because in the narrative he states that in 1846, when he was forty-
five years of age, he retired to a place called Campestre and thence
to Santa María de la Boca del Monte. It is assumed that these two

places are in Paraguay, first because the names are in Spanish, and second because he claims to have entered Argentina by way of Paraguay.

The mention the Hermit makes of a mineral spring with "wonderful curative properties," indicates that he never professed to be a healer, although the people who benefited by the baths and herbs he prescribed attributed the results to his personal virtues.

> Ignorant people began to think that the cure produced by the water and the natural remedies I gave them were the effects of my own personal holiness, and I had to leave the place to escape their constant visits and their too great honors.

In looking over the Hermit's story, it is difficult to reconcile his constant insistence upon being let alone and at the same time his seeking out important personages wherever he went, whose courtesies he refuses as "too great honors." In turning down the ordination offered him by various bishops, he speaks of a vow he must keep but nowhere does he tell us what the vow consists of, although we assume it is one of solitude. Despite these inconsistencies, the places and people he mentions are usually geographically and historically correct.

But, to go on with the story of his wanderings. He crossed over into Argentina by way of Paraguay and reached Buenos Aires on August 31, 1853. He speaks of visiting the dictator Rosas, who received him with great honors; but he could not refrain from condemning the tyrant's misdeeds, and as a result he had to move to the pampas and to the "Comanche Indians." Apparently the scribe or copyist confused the Indians of the Argentine pampa with those of the American Southwest, for there are no Comanches in Argentina. Also Rosas was exiled to England in 1852.

Shortly after leaving the Argentine capital, the Hermit took passage on a French boat up the Paraná River to Rosario, but a few days later the boat developed engine trouble and he was forced to abandon ship. The enterprising traveler then bought a horse and continued on his way for several days, until one night when he was camping in the desert someone came along and stole his mount. Apparently at that time of his life he was not as insistent on walking as he was ten years later when he walked from Council Grove, Kansas, to Las Vegas, New Mexico. The next entry in his narrative skips over the rest of the journey, until he reached the city of Mendoza on the eastern slopes of the Andes, where he found another cave about four leagues out of town. Father Daniel Baez, Superior of the Convent of Our Lady of Saint Francis, wrote on May 1, 1854, a letter included in his folder:

> Don Juan de Agostini chose to follow his vocation to the west of the city where he persevered in the most austere, humble and penitent life till he was driven out of his cave by the terrible weather of our winter season.

In the spring of 1854 the Hermit had not yet found the peace of mind he was searching for; and so he crossed over into Chile and continued his quest farther south into the province of Talca. A few months later he retraced his steps northward as far as La Serena, where he once more debated with himself the advisability of taking orders and staying to preach to the Indians of the desert. Not even his confessor, Bishop Don Justo Donoso, was able to convince him; hence he picked up his few belongings and departed for Bolivia.

While in Chile, the Hermit went through the spiritual crisis of his life, to judge by the correspondence he had with Bishop Donoso. In one of these letters he writes that his "conscience has been ill at ease" since leaving La Serena, and adds: "If you think me fit, you may ordain me, . . ." No sooner had this letter gone out, than he changed his mind and wrote another one telling the Bishop that he felt no inclination toward the priesthood and besides, dreaded the responsibilities more than anything else in the world. He also mentioned the "vows of chastity and poverty as a religious of Saint Anthony Abbott," which he must keep and from which no one could release him.

Mr. Baca of Santa Fe and others who had direct information about the Hermit have always insisted that he did not believe in the sacraments and that he was at odds with some of the doctrine of the Church. In writing to Bishop Donoso he was distressed and undecided about accepting orders. He seemed to be very fond of his confessor, and would have liked to stay with him "as long as your Grace lives." Yet, he turned down the invitation saying: "I could not live with the indispensable obligations of the priest to preach and administer the sacraments." At this time also he spoke of having dropped the "habit of monastic life . . . on account of some persons, may God forgive them!" He must have gone back to it when he was in the United States; the photographs he had taken in New York and the ones made in Las Vegas, New Mexico show him with a cape and cowl.

Still in a quandry about his spiritual life, Maria de Agostini, as he signed his name at that time, took counsel with the Franciscans in La Paz. He mentions José Nerva O.F.M., and Father Mariano Sánchez, both of whom tried unsuccessfully to persuade him to enter the ministry to "be useful first to the Catholic Apostolic and Roman religion, second to the human family, and finally to the State."

He took up his abode on Mount Illimani in a cave, as was his custom, and went down on Sundays to the city. It was while traveling in this high country that he felt the heavy hand of persecution for the first time.

Coming to a village I was arrested by order of the Corregidor who was a drunkard and a man of loose morals. Meanwhile they stole all my possessions; a travelling bag, some Chilean coins, religious pictures and medals . . . The good people of the village gave me a bad horse and saddle and I escaped from that den of thieves.

Disgusted with the reception he had been given in Bolivia, the Hermit went around Lake Titicaca and reached the city of Arequipa in southern Peru. One cannot call the record kept by the old man a diary because he skips several years or several hundred miles of travel unless something important or unusual happened to him or around him. After leaving Arequipa he simply states: "I had been twenty-one years in South America." From this, we infer that the date for his departure to Central America, his next stop, was about 1859.

He spent "only nine months in the Jenet Mountains of Central America," and then decided to try his luck on Mount Orizaba in southern Mexico. He picked out a spot "above timberline and very well suited for my purpose." Soon he was being visited not only by the Indians but by many others in the region who brought him fruits, sugar, rice, and other supplies. This incited the jealousy of the government, according to the Hermit, and it was not long before a detachment of the famous Mexican Mounted Police, the *Rurales* took him into custody. Apparently the solitary man had not fared so badly here, if the list of confiscated goods is an indication:

They stole more than seven hundred pesos worth of things from me, on the way from Orizaba to Puebla. In coin they took twenty-four pesos and the rest in various articles such as lamps, wax, shirts, and other clothing, and tools for my personal use."

He did not last long in Mexico—the country was inhospitable to him—and before the end of the year the authorities put him on a boat at the port of Veracruz headed for Havana. This was in October of 1861.

Despite the constant claims that he was not interested in the things of this world, the Hermit was somewhat of a posturer and had no mean opinion of himself. This may have been what was at the bottom of his constant struggle and his restlessness. Moreover, it may also have been one of the reasons why he refused to be ordained. Had he accepted the habit he would have lost his independence and disappeared into anonymity.

The Hermit was not an autograph collector, but he had the good fortune to collect letters of recommendation from prominent people, which he used very effectively as passports or to get out of difficult situations. Important-looking documents and *recomendaciones* from higher officials are indispensable in Latin America even today; hence it may well be that the Hermit learned this detail soon after he arrived in Caracas. When he started for New Mexico—to get ahead of our story—he was carrying a letter of introduction from the commander of the American garrison at Council Grove, Kansas, and he presented it to Don Manuel Romero as his wagon train was about to pull out on the Santa Fe Trail. In Cuba the letters of recommendation he salvaged from the things stolen in Mexico were used to good advantage:

> Thanks to my many letters of recommendation, I was welcomed in the Cuban capital, and everybody treated me with respect. In fact, someone having taken my picture sold plenty of them, as each one was anxious to possess a souvenir from "The Marvel of our Century"!

The fortunes of the poor Hermit had been on the wane from the time he entered Bolivia. In Mexico he was deported to what he first thought to be a good land, but apparently he was so accustomed to living in cold climates that he could not withstand the sultry, low altitude of the tropics. In thinking of a country where he could once more breathe the rarified atmosphere of the mountains, he decided on Quebec, a Catholic country, and went there by way of the United States. But things did not turn out well:

> My ragged clothes and my mean appearance did not appeal to the Canadians. The cold climate seemed to have congealed the heart of its inhabitants, and I soon found out that my ignorance of the French language, which I understood but could not speak, would work against me. . . . . It was the saddest period of my life.

At this juncture he was so unhappy that he even thought of returning to Italy, although for some unknown reason he had vowed never to go back to his native land. Very succinctly he expressed his decision: "Finally, I decided to go west."

CHAPTER 13

THE HERMIT'S TRAIL
TO NEW MEXICO

◆

IT IS QUITE LIKELY that nothing would have been known about Juan Maria Agostini, the Hermit, had he not turned up early one morning at the wagon camp of a Santa Fe trader by the name of Don Manuel Romero, who was getting ready to start back to New Mexico from Council Grove, Kansas. Don Manuel was *mayordomo* and part owner of one of the ox trains that plied back and forth on the Santa Fe Trail. On the morning of May 28, 1863, he was getting his teamsters ready for the long trek across the western plains when an old man with a flowing white beard, and wearing a long, black cape over his stooped shoulders, approached him. As travelers seeking passage to the West during Civil War days were no novelty to Don Manuel, he was not surprised at the stranger's request to join the caravan.

Mr. Romero's attention was drawn to the old man before him, however, when he read the letter handed him by way of introduction. Here the commander of the garrison at Council Grove stated that the bearer, Juan Maria Agustiniani, was a person of good character, a missionary to the Indians, who had lived in caves elsewhere subsisting entirely on vegetable foods. More surprising still was the old man's refusal to ride in one of the wagons when given the privilege of doing so by the trader. Very politely he explained: "All I want is the privilege of accompany-

ing you to the mountains of the West. I prefer to walk, thank you sir."

Thus began the close friendship between the rugged plainsman and the equally rugged, though delicate-appearing Hermit, which was to last to the end of their respective days. Mr. Romero also became the link with the old man's past, and later the reference source for historians, folklorists, and all persons interested in the legends that grew around the recluse. The overland trip

was punctuated with the usual routine of land travel common in those days. The only reference made to the Hermit during the weeks on the road was his ministering to those who took sick, and the administering of the last rites to one of the members of the train who died along the way.

Indian country had to be crossed, but Indians were a familiar sight to a man like Juan Agostini who had spent more than two decades in Latin America. During the many weeks of plodding along dusty, hot plains he became accustomed to the folkways of the people with whom he was going west to live; and it may well be that this close association was instrumental in his decision to end his wanderings. As the train moved on, the old man already past his sixtieth year, walked alongside of Don Manuel's horse and revealed to him in conversation some of the events of his interesting life.

Every morning the Hermit raised his staff in greeting to the mounted scouts who went ahead every day in search of a good campsite and water for the stock. When scouts of an outgoing train met those of an oncoming caravan, they would select a suitable location for the two companies to spend the night together. These joint meetings helped to break the monotony for the traders and gave the Hermit a good opportunity to understand the customs of Western Americans. It also provided travelers and families at home with a means of communication. The trains from New Mexico brought letters for the trains they met along the way, and also brought news of babies born, marriages, deaths, and the general welfare of families not seen in months.

The traders with New Mexican products to sell, and those returning with supplies from the east profited by discussing market conditions and salable stock at these joint meetings. There was also fun and entertainment. The returning trains were well supplied with two luxuries very much in demand, sugar and coffee; and the men from New Mexico had homemade beverages to use for barter. Moreover, each outfit was well supplied with at least one troubadour, who in addition to his repertoire of homespun *trovos* and *canciones* could improvise in facile verse appropriate ballads for every occasion. When the business of the day was over and the oxen had been safely put out to graze, *mancornados* so they would not stray too far from camp, the coffeepots were put on the coals, the jug was passed around, and the men gathered to hear the traditional singers from each train vie with each other singing *décimas, corridos,* and *inditas* until one of them emerged victorious. Sometimes these contests lasted until sunrise.[1]

The caravan led by Don Manuel Romero finally arrived at the cluster of houses that was the Las Vegas of that day. One of the principal homes of the village was that of the well-to-do trader, and into it he brought the old Hermit as his guest. It was the end of one more business trip for Don Manuel, and the end of a quest for solitude for a religious man who had started in northern Italy in 1827 to satisfy an inward desire to be at peace with himself. Still true to his vow, the Hermit refused the rich and highly spiced food served by the Romero household in celebration of a successful trading expedition. He requested simply a dish of *atole,* a corn meal mush or gruel of Mexican (Aztec) origin commonly used by the Spanish-Americans up to the time of World War I. It's a very nourishing dish prepared in a number of ways with cinnamon and brown sugar, out of parched corn or from *masa,* a dough made from ground boiled corn.

The Hermit did not tarry long at the home of Don Manuel Romero, but in the short time he was there word spread through the nearby villages that a holy man had come into town from afar. The benign aspect of the blackrobed old man leaning on a staff wherever he went, his willingness to give counsel, and the story of his travels appealed to the religious nature of the New Mexican peasants. They saw in this anchorite the reappearance of one of the Biblical prophets, and looked to him for guidance and advice. In spite of his eccentricities the Hermit must have been a kindly man and a good man, for he has continued to live

[1] Arthur L. Campa, *Los Comanches: A New Mexican Folk Drama,* University of New Mexico *Bulletin,* Modern Language Series, Vol. VII, No. 1 (April, 1942).

in the memory of the villages around Las Vegas for almost a century. To this day, no one has ever said anything but good about him.

In the days when the healing arts were essentially nothing more than advice and the application of a few household remedies, the experienced Hermit acquired the reputation of a healer, and was sought out by countless unfortunates suffering from chronic and incurable diseases. The persistent crowds soon drove him out of Las Vegas in search of a place where he might escape the company of his fellow men. Several miles southeast of the village, where Romeroville now stands, he came to a natural cave on the east wall of the canyon, and there once more he took up the anchorite life he had led for almost half a century. But here too the people from Rosiada, Gallinas, and San Geronimo discovered his retreat and came to him in increasing numbers. Not only did they call on him, but they pitched tents and windbreaks near the cave in order to enjoy the beneficent influence of "El Santo Ermitaño."

In the summer of 1952 I visited many of these villages and was astonished at the number of stories told by the mountaineers about the miraculous powers of "El Ermitaño Juan Bautista." There was a woman by the name of Domitilia Martínez, whose grandfather had known the Hermit quite well, and had been one of the men who later went to the Peak to build a cabin for him. She talked at length about the Hermit as though she had known him personally, an attitude still in evidence among the villagers around Las Vegas. She mentioned the tinkling bell on his walking staff and how he used to bring the people together with its beckoning sound. After conducting religious services in his own manner, he would prescribe stewed potions and rubefacients to ailing patients. The faith people had in his suggestions must have had a psychological effect upon the sufferers with no doubt favorable results, and these "cures" grew by a natural process into miracles of healing.

Don Hipólito Baca strongly denied that the Hermit had, or ever claimed to have, any healing powers or that he performed miracles.

"People say that he performed miracles, but that isn't so. He was a religious man, but since he did not believe in the sacraments he could not have been given the power to perform miracles. All the Hermit ever wanted was to live in solitude."

The acts of kindness performed by Juan Maria Agostini at the present Romeroville brought on him such a crowd that he soon began to think of a new, far-off place where he might avoid this intrusion. Skylighted against the western horizon he saw a mountain peak that appealed to him in the Sangre de Cristo Range. It was far removed from village traffic and conducive to meditation. One day without any warning he merely announced he was leaving the Romeroville Canyon. He picked up his satchel of papers, swung a small bag of corn meal over his shoulder, and started north for Las Vegas leaning on his walking staff. When he arrived at the village, he called on his good friend Don Manuel Romero and told him of his plan to seek a place to live on Cerro del Tecolote as the Peak was called at that time. He set his course west, up the Gallinas Canyon, and reached El Porvenir deep in the mountains by the end of the second day. On the third day he reached the top of the first mountain ridge, and through the tops of the pine trees he caught sight of his objective.

The lofty mountain, the mystic beauty of which is suggestive of the Himalayan peaks where dwell the holy lamas, stood out against the blue sky, with a low-hanging mist for a crown over its rugged top. Juan Maria Agostini observed the double-headed cliff, his future home, from where he stood, and studied the path he would follow to reach the summit. It was a long climb for a man past his sixtieth birthday, but the doughty little Hermit was determined, and besides he was used to walking in the mountains. Slowly he made his way through the thickly timbered slopes, over game trails leading to the top from the west side, and eventually was able to breathe the thin air of New Mexico's rarified atmosphere on top of Owl's Peak. From the vantage point of his new abode he surveyed the valleys below and saw the trail that had brought him to the west disappear on the horizon. The only company he had now was the twittering blue jays, the magpie with its raucous call, and the screaming eagles circling their nest on the cliffs of Tecolote. Juan Maria Agostini had searched for privacy and solitude, and now he found them, surrounded by unparalleled beauty.

About three hundred feet below the eastern side of the Peak, the Hermit selected a hollowed cave, which provided him shelter from the heavy winter snows, and offered cover from the thunderstorms that lash the mountain top in summer. Inside this open cave, moisture dropped into a hole he dug in the floor, providing all the water necessary for his needs. Many years after his death, the dripping from the ceiling of his abandoned cave slowed to an occasional drop, and the villagers claim that anyone able to catch three drops on the tip of the tongue will forever tell the truth. One wag insists that the reason these mountaineers can tell the truth only partially is that no one has ever caught more than two drops.

When I visited the cave in 1953, it had already become a sort of shrine where friends of the Hermit and the *Sociedad del Ermitaño* journey to pay tribute to the saintly old man who, although not authorized by the Catholic Church, had provided spiritual comfort and physical well-being to the people in the villages around his lofty retreat. The niches in the cave were filled with images and religious pictures, and at the entrance was an

old timber cross weathered by the elements but still a silent reminder of the man who almost a hundred years past had lived
in these simple premises alone.

Even the remoteness of this peak did not keep some of his
friends from calling on him, and when they saw the rustic, primitive shelter he was living in they brought axes and felled trees
with which to build a windbreak in front of the cave, which
would also protect him at night from the prowling cougar and
intrusive black bears.

The Hermit stayed on the mountain most of the time and
came down to the surrounding villages only when his supply
of corn meal was low. On these trips he sold crucifixes and
beads he had fashioned from the soft white pine of the forest,
and attended to the spiritual needs of his friends. By now everyone realized that the old man wanted to be left alone, but they
felt sorry for the way in which he had to live, with nothing but
a windbreak and a cave to protect him from the hard winters.
One day a group of volunteers arrived on top of the peak with
axes, spades, and other building tools, and announced to the
Hermit that they were going to build a nice cabin for him.

The dripping spring in the cave was enough for the Hermit,
but hardly enough for a group of workers, whose needs were
much greater. When they ran out of water, it is said that the
Hermit walked over to one of the rocks along the cliff and
touched it with his staff, and that a spring of crystalline water
gushed forth. There are many other versions as to how the
mountain spring came into being. Some say that a young sheepherder climbed to the top of Tecolote Mountain while he grazed
his sheep on the slopes below and accidentally ran across the
Hermit. While he was visiting with the old man, the boy asked
him for a drink, whereupon the Hermit told him to fill his can-
teen at a spring between two pine trees standing before them.

The lad knew of no spring on the mountain and simply looked incredulously at his newly found friend thinking probably that the old man was a little *loco*. The Hermit insisted that he try the spring, and to his great surprise he found a bubbling spring of fresh water.

Don Hipólito Baca insisted that all these stories about the Hermit's bringing forth water by touching a rock with his staff were nothing but delusions of the folk, or at best, Biblical throwbacks confused in the minds of people.

"No, no, there was no such thing! There is a spring on top of the peak, and the people built the cabin right over it so the Hermit would not have to go out to get water. That same spring has always been there. I remember as a young boy I used to go up there with other kids from Las Vegas and we all would drink from the spring. The funny thing about it is that the water does not run anywhere. There is no stream running from it. It goes right back into the ground."

Don Hipólito was right. I rode a horse to the top of Hermit's Peak and watered it at the spring, where traces of the cabin were still visible. There were also the crosses leading to the original cave overlooking the valley towards Las Vegas and three large ones on the edge of the cliff.

Getting back to the story. While the workmen were building the cabin for the Hermit, the old man insisted on feeding them a very tasty stew he had prepared for them. No matter how many servings were taken from the pot, it never gave out during the time they were with him. These and many other stories are still told about the good old Hermit of Tecolote.

According to all accounts, the cabin was built without any doors or windows. There was one opening barely large enough for the Hermit to squeeze through. Some say that he had the men drive spikes all around the inside of the opening in order to worry the flesh every time he used it, but others disagree with this version saying that the spikes were placed there simply to keep out wild animals. There is also a story about a large log, which the Hermit placed between two crags over a two-thousand-foot precipice in order to remind him as he walked across it daily "of the uncertainty of life." Most of these stories suggest penance in some form or another, probably because so much of this sort of thing has been seen among the Penitentes of New Mexico. There is a marked tendency among writers today to appeal to readers by making badmen very bad, gunmen too handy with a forty-five, and Penitentes very secretive and dangerous. This same tendency prevails when speaking of the Hermit; he is everything from a saint to a flagellant.

It has been pretty well established through informed sources that the *Via Crucis* attributed to the Penitente Society was put up by friends of the Hermit who formed the *Sociedad del Ermitaño,* that the ax-hewn crosses along the trail and on top of the Peak were the monument which these men placed there for their old friend. This informal Society or Brotherhood makes pilgrimages in May and September to the Hermit's cave to commemorate the recluse's life of service. The object is simple devotion to a good friend and is in no way connected with Penitente rites. In a land where penance and flagellation are commonly practiced, the Hermit's eccentricities may have been interpreted as penance, and as a result many forms of self-inflicted punishment may have been attributed to him.

One point on which there has always been a consensus is the Hermit's deep and sincere concern for the welfare of others. One cannot help admiring the fortitude of an aged man who could walk twenty miles from his lofty perch on a mountain top to the surrounding valleys in all kinds of weather and under conditions that would try the hardiest pioneer. He made no distinction among people, the rich and the poor were his friends, and no one ever turned him out. The home of his friend and benefactor, Manuel Romero, was usually the first he visited when he was in Las Vegas, but he also visited the family of Teodoro Peña where Peterson Reservoir now stands, and at the home of the Major Morrison, where he could have had the best room in the house and enjoyed the hospitality of his table. The old man refused all these attentions; he chose to eat the plain corn gruel to which he had become accustomed, and slept upon bare boards or earthen floors. According to Mr. Schoonmacher, the Hermit "never removed the leather shirt which he wore, having pointed tacks driven through it from the outer side, when he slept on the floor." Members of the Romero-Baca family have no knowledge of this and dismiss the story as a "figment of the imagination."

The Hermit may not have been a Penitente, such as may be found in the mountains of New Mexico, but being a deeply religious man it is very likely that he practiced the usual penances known among members of the Roman Catholic Church. The very fact that he lived on such a tasteless diet of corn gruel, and his insistence upon walking wherever he went, and sleeping on bare floors indicate a form of corporal mortification not far removed from actual penance. The posse that found him dead in the Organ Mountains brought back a *cilicios* or spiked belt he was wearing when murdered. This may have been what Rodney Schoonmacher had in mind when he spoke of the leather shirt with pointed tacks.

The impression one gathers from reading what the Hermit had to say about his life, his aspirations, and his relations with other people, is that he had an inward struggle from the time he left Italy until he died. He was restless, constantly searching for something which he did not altogether find, running away from something he never disclosed, wanting to be alone and yet seeking company. When he lived on Tecolote Mountain he arranged with Samuel B. Watrous, the New Mexican pioneer after whom the town of that name is known today, that he would light a fire on top of the Peak every third day as a signal that all was well with him.

For almost five years he stood the rigors of the mountain winters and enjoyed the friendship of all the mountain villages around Las Vegas, but a man who had been on the move since 1830 could not stay in one place, even on the Peak where he had found comparative solitude and retirement. Once again without any ceremony he simply announced to his sorrowing friends that Mexico beckoned to him, and that he must obey the calling. So, in answer to that inner urge to travel which had always motivated him, he picked up his scant belongings and started on his journey southward, his last one over the Spanish Trail. Those who were not too well informed wrote later that the Indians killed him somewhere near Socorro. Others say that he was overtaken by robbers, who thought he had gold in his corn meal bag and murdered him. Actually, he was not molested along the four-hundred-mile trek to the Organ Mountains near the present city of Las Cruces. He reached the village of Mesilla close to the Mexican border, but did not cross into the country where he had been so inhospitably treated several years before.

In the spring of 1867 he arrived in Old Mesilla and sought out the principal resident, Colonel Albert Fountain. Some writers picture his arrival in somewhat Hollywood fashion and evoke a scene like this:

"The tall man, clad in a ragged Confederate uniform and clerical cape and cowl, paused to raise the crucifix in salutation. It could be no other than El Ermitaño, stories of whose miracles now followed the trail. . . . and so it came about that Juan Maria Agustiniana, the once little lad of Lombardy, rode comfortably into Mesilla as the revered guest of the prominent Gonzalez family."

The description given above is an imaginative portrayal of

what probably never happened. For one thing, the Hermit was far from being a "tall man," and he always wore a simple pair of trousers with a cape and hood over his shoulders. The photographs taken in New York and in Las Vegas always show him dressed in this manner, and the description given everywhere his legend is known speaks of nothing but this simple garb. Furthermore, it is not likely that a man who chose to walk from Council Grove, Kansas, and had walked almost four hundred miles from Las Vegas to Mesilla would accept a ride just as he was approaching a new village. His flowing beard, his cape and cowl, and the tinkling of the bell attached to his walking staff would make a far more impressive entry than riding in some stranger's wagon.

As was usually the case, wherever the Hermit lived, numerous stories grew out of his eccentric habits, and also from the fact that no one knew exactly who he was. Through his own chronicle, we know that people misinterpreted his healing ability and declared that he worked miracles, but though he well knew his own limitations he was no shrinking violet and probably was to some degree responsible for the legends that grew about him.

While he was in Mesilla it is told that he continued to give advice and counsel to those who requested it. His long years of travel over many lands in the days when travel was uncommon, and his knowledge of several languages raised him to the stature of a wiseman among the unlettered, and made him an interesting conversationalist among the better educated. Even though he was not in complete accord with all aspects of Roman Catholic theology, he was a nominal Catholic and thus represented a religion that is traditional among most New Mexicans. No one outside of the clergy could understand his disagreement with Church doctrine, and so the folk by and large took him for what he appeared to be: an eccentric old anchorite.

Some say that the Hermit went beyond Mesilla as far as San Antonio, Texas. They may mean the village of San Antonio de Senecu just a few miles below El Paso. The only known contemporary evidence of his travel beyond the mountains around El Paso is contained in a short news story that appeared in the *Galveston Tri-Weekly News* of March 18, 1867:

> A hermit has taken up his abode in the Apache country, in the Hueco Mountains, about thirty-five miles east of El Paso. He is an Italian by birth, about sixty years of age, speaks many languages, is well educated, and is believed by the simple Mexicans, who visit him by the hundreds, to be endowed with remarkable gifts, such as working of miracles, etc. He has resided in Peru among the Andes, in Brazil, Patagonia, Central America, and subsequently in Europe and Asia, and also in the Pyrenees, and more recently among the mountains of New Mexico.

This short newspaper account sums up pretty much what is known about the Hermit even today, as well as what is said about him in popular tradition. After his sojourn down the Río Grande, he returned to the Organ Mountains, found another cave in a place known today as La Cueva, and once again took up his troglodytal existence. In the relatively short time he spent in these mountains, he became known to the few people who lived up and down the Río Grande Valley. He sought out the most important families, as was his custom, not because he needed any of the physical comforts they could afford him, but perhaps because he enjoyed the company of cultured people. Colonel Fountain was a close friend of the Romeros, in whose company he had come to New Mexico, therefore he always visited this home whenever he came down from his mountain retreat. The descendants of the Fountain family of 1869 are the ones who know the last chapter of his life. This family has in its possession many of the personal effects owned by him when he was found dead near his cave.

Once again Juan Maria Agostini proposed to Colonel Fountain the fire signals, which he had used on the Peak near Las Vegas with Mr. Watrous, in order to advise him that he was alive and well. This time the plan served its tragic purpose. On the third night towards the end of April of 1869, no signal fires were seen on the slopes of the Organs. When the Hermit did not come into the village the next day, Colonel Fountain realizing that something was wrong organized a posse consisting of Sheriff Mariano Barela of Doña Ana County, Pedro Onopa, Antonio Garcia, and Rodrigo Ruelas, and went up to investigate. They did not have far to search. They found the old recluse lying prostrate on the ground with a dagger thrust in his back, the victim of someone who apparently knew his living habits. It was surmised by the posse that he had been attacked while he was on his knees, probably in prayer. Robbery was not the motive, for none of his personal belongings had been taken; neither was it very likely that the Indians had waylaid him, for they would have gone through his things and probably would have scalped him. To this day no one knows why an old man whose only interest was to live alone and help his friends when he visited the village, should have come to such a tragic end.

In the ninety-odd years that have elapsed since the Hermit's murder numerous conjectures have been advanced, not only as to why he was killed but as to how he met his death. Some say that his body was pierced with arrows, thus suggesting an Indian attack. Others claim that he was badly mutilated by sword thrusts. The most interesting recent account is the one that appeared in the April 30, 1953, issue of the *Las Cruces Citizen*: "The murderers attacked the Holy One while he slept, as he had only his underwear clothes on his body." This story assumes that the Hermit undressed when he lay down to sleep in the barrenness of his lonely cave, a most unlikely habit for a man whose design for living was not physical comfort.

The fact remains that no one has been able to determine conclusively who was responsible for the death of Juan Maria Agostini. There are widespread rumors that the Catholic Church was not in sympathy with his religious practices, and that the local clergy wherever he went resented his popularity among their parishioners, but it is hard to believe that even the strongest feeling against him would have led to murder.

Published records give two different dates for the Hermit's death. George Griggs, an Old Mesilla pioneer, tells us in his *History of the Mesilla Valley and the Gadsden Purchase* that he died on April 17, 1869. The *Río Grande Republican* of June 30, 1869, published a list of "Indian Depredations Committed in 1869 near Las Cruces" in which is found the following entry: "April 29, Italian hermit killed in Organ Mountains, Doña Ana County, (near Cuervo Ranch)."

In Mesilla I visited the old Fountain home, and Mrs. Elizabeth Armendariz, granddaughter of the Colonel, showed me the collection of articles belonging to the Hermit, which were left as part of the museum of her grandfather. One of the most interesting items was the belt with sharp spikes, which the Hermit is supposed to have worn at all times. These belts are known as *cilicios* in Spanish, but properly speaking they are not that at all; *cilicios* are horsehair belts or shirts worn next to the flesh, something comparable to the sackcloth of Biblical days. Other articles such as books, a rosary, and the famous little bell that the Hermit carried on his walking staff were on loan to Father Kupper. Later in the week I saw them, together with some of the autobiographical material previously mentioned.

Since up to that time nothing had been said about "El Ermitaño's" grave, it occurred to me to inquire if anyone knew where he was buried. Elizabeth Armendariz said she could show it to me provided the markers had not disintegrated after so many years. We went to the cemetery and looked around until we came to a flat slab overgrown with weeds. It was badly weathered and crumbling, but part of an indistinct inscription could be read on it. Outside of the descendants of the Fountain family, there are hardly any Old Mesilla residents who know about the Hermit. This is probably due to the fact that he lived in that part of the country for a relatively short time. About a year after my visit a story in the *Las Cruces Citizen* quoted an inscription supposedly placed on the Hermit's grave at the time of his death.

> Juan Maria Justiniano, Hermitano del Viejo y Nuevo Mundo. El murio dia del 17 de Abril, ano de 1869 a los 69 anos de edad y los de 49 de Hermitano.

It is not very likely that a man of the education and culture of Colonel Fountain would have allowed so incorrectly written an inscription to be placed on the grave of his good friend. Moreover, the New Mexicans of 1869 would not have committed such glaring and impossible errors in Spanish, for these errors are not common to Spanish-speaking writers.

The legend of the Hermit of Las Vegas, by whatever name he may be called, will continue to live and grow in New Mexican tradition so long as the double-headed mountain stands as a lasting monument to a kind old Italian anchorite who, in his own peculiar way brought help and comfort to the mountain folk and provided entertaining company to his peers. A trip to the Peak is a rewarding experience on foot and a real treat on horseback, riding over winding mountain trails through the stately pines where, as Omar Barker says:

> Columbines bloom and mule deer feed and the cougar prowling its crag at night can see the lights of Las Vegas eighteen miles away.

CHAPTER 14

Indians and Spaniards

◆

One of the difficult problems faced by the early Spanish settlers of the upper Río Grande was that of living peaceably with the Indian tribes surrounding their villages and rancherias. From Texas to Arizona, settlers were constantly harassed by surprise attacks and kept on the alert by the imminent threat of Indian raids. The Indians in turn suffered the reprisals resulting from this frontier warfare, but these counter-attacks did not lessen their enthusiasm. This unhealthy state of Indian-settler relations made each wary of the other, and the settler, who was essentially an agriculturist, tried to reduce the dangers of armed conflict by converting the Indians to Roman Catholicism or by keeping on sufficiently good terms with them to carry on trade and barter operations. This was more readily accomplished among those living in communal pueblos, but there was less success with the roaming tribes of Comanches, Apaches, and Navajos who depended partially on pillage for their subsistence.

Almost to the end of the nineteenth century there was intermittent warfare consisting mainly of Indian raids followed by punitive expeditions sent out to rescue captives and to retrieve stolen stock. As a result of these incursions, the territory surrounding the settlements became a sort of no man's land where no one ventured alone for very long. The seminomadic tribes

considered settlers as intruders upon their domain, and when unable to trade for the provisions they raised, the Indians tried to wrest food from them in order to subsist. This story has been told and retold by historians, novelists, and poets. Even the popular bards and folk playwriters have fashioned ballads and dramas out of the spectacular conflict. In the Taos valley of northern New Mexico, the peasants still enact the Comanche dances as a grim reminder of what once was a fear-inspiring spectacle. They also enact a traditional play, in which Cuerno Verde, a Comanche chief of the eighteenth century, is slain in battle. The characters are all historical personages but in traditional transmission they have acquired the stature of legendary heroes.

Occasionally there were romantic sequels arising from the contact of Indian and settler in the Southwest, not too different from the Pocahontas episode though hardly as well embellished by royal recognition and social status. The "romance" was usually forced by the suitor on one side, often with fatal results.

Josiah Gregg mentions an interesting case, which he prefaces with the statement that "The first white settler of Taos was a Spaniard named Pando." According to this story, the father of the Pando family about 1745 was greatly concerned over the Comanche threat to his hacienda, and in order to keep on good terms with this warlike tribe he promised to give his daughter in marriage to a chief when she should become of age. For many years he harvested his crops unmolested and eventually became a prosperous landholder, but when the Indian finally came to claim his bride after she grew up, she refused to have anything to do with the young chief assigned to her. The Comanches in reprisal for the broken bargain, destroyed the hacienda and killed all members of the family except the girl, whom they carried away to the plains. They seem to have had little interest in the not-to-be bride and sold her to the Pawnees, who in turn traded her to a Frenchman from St. Louis. It is said that some very distinguished families in southern Missouri claimed to be the proud descendants of the unfortunate bartered bride of the Pando household.

A legend similar to the one related by Gregg, and much

better authenticated in New Mexican tradition, centers around a family by the name of Baca that used to live in the little village of Tomé, a few miles south of Albuquerque. The town was first established in 1740 by the *Genízaros* when they became displeased at the treatment they received from the Spaniards. These "Janizaries" were Indians of various tribes taken from their tribal enemies and resettled by the Spaniards, who often used them as allies against other Indians. In 1767 Don Ignacio Baca settled with his family in the vicinity of Tomé and in a few years developed his land holdings into a good-sized hacienda. By this time the Comanches who roamed the plains adjacent to Tomé had gained considerable mobility through their acquisition of the horse from the Spaniards, and moved freely over the West trading or warring with white men and Indians alike. A very substantial business was carried on by pioneer traveling salesmen developed in New Mexico and called *Comancheros*. These daring traders met at appointed places with the Comanches and traded regularly for pelts and stolen stock paid for in gunpowder and firearms.

When the Comanches were not trading, they raided the smaller communities where no garrisons were stationed, and Tomé with its small population was vulnerable to these attacks. One day these Indians made a sudden appearance in the village, and as the chief rode into the plaza he was attracted by Don Ignacio Baca's little daughter playing in front of the church. He immediately proposed to the Spanish settler that when the girl grew up she should be married to his son, and Don Ignacio willing to be at peace with the dangerous chief agreed to the bargain, thinking that by the time little María grew up the Indian would have forgotten the affair.

According to one of the many variants of the legend, the Comanches visited the household of Don Ignacio each year and brought him horses and cattle, which they had probably stolen from other ranches of the West. The hacienda prospered, and eventually María grew into a very attractive young girl. The day of reckoning came, however, when the Comanche chief called at the home of Don Ignacio accompanied by his son in full tribal regalia ready to claim the bride he had been promised when he was a boy. The Spaniard, who at one time had thought he was satisfying an Indian's passing fancy, realized the seriousness of the original proposal, but having no intention of letting his daughter become the bride of a roaming barbarian, he hid María for several days and with heavy heart informed the old chief that his daughter had died that year.

The disappointed father and son, satisfied with Don Ignacio's explanation, left the hacienda and returned to the plains. Some say that a neighboring Isleta Indian told the Comanches that the story about María's death was a hoax designed to keep the girl from marrying the chief's son. When they learned this, the Comanches returned to Tomé and wiped out the settlement after a bloody battle. Only María was spared, but she was taken by her original suitor; and tradition says that despite the tragedy that befell her family she lived happily and had many children, whose descendants still bear the name of Baca and claim to be of the original stock of Don Ignacio Baca of Tomé. In April of 1954, eight skulls were unearthed in the modern village of Tomé which, according to Isidoro Armijo now living there, are supposed to be the remains of the settlers who perished in the sacking of Tomé a century and a half earlier.

Many years after María Baca was abducted from her little home town, the Comanches returned once more; but this time they were not so fortunate as they had been before. They were met east of Tomé on a round-topped hill known today as Cerro de Tomé but better known in years past as Cerro del Canadá. (Hubert Howe Bancroft believes that the name of Canada was given to the hill by a group of Canadians who settled there in

1840.) When the people of Tomé saw the size of the Comanche encampment, they decided to make a daring proposal to the chief through a spokesman named Juan Chávez, which is like saying John Smith in English. Don Juan rode into the Comanche camp and asked to see the chief. Thinking that the settler came to ask for surrender terms, the Indian leader had him brought to his tipi immediately. The farmer surprised the chief with his strange proposal. Said he, "You have brought many warriors to fight a small village with no more than a hundred men able to bear arms." Then, hoping to appeal to the vanity of the Comanche chief, he added:

"The Comanche is known as a brave and able warrior in the West. Let him prove it today in the field of battle. You can easily overwhelm us with such a large force and add nothing to your prestige. Let fifty of your picked warriors meet an equal number of our men from Tomé on top of this hill and the outcome of this fight will decide the battle."

The Comanche Chief, accustomed to hand-to-hand combat, was pleased at the prospect of battle and agreed to lead fifty of his braves against an equal number of settlers. The Indians withdrew to the north side of the hill to watch the fight, and the settlers arrayed themselves on the south side overlooking their village towards the Río Grande. At the agreed signal both sides spurred their horses into battle. The Indians attacked with a fearsome war whoop abetted by the heavy beat of tom-toms, and the settlers rushed at the enemy with a loud "Santiago!" the battle cry of Spaniards since the year 711.

Sword and lance, tomahawk and battle-ax met with a clash. Arrows filled the air, and occasional bursts of firearms took their toll as the combatants came to grips at close quarters. The struggle became confused; the horsemen closed upon each other, and the warlike Comanches began to push back the settlers fighting for their homes. The settlers lacked the leadership that the Indians, accustomed to combat, had in their chiefs. Suddenly a Spaniard mounted on a white war horse rallied them and led them back into the thick of battle. Their new leader opened the way through the Indian fighters crashing his mighty sword on enemy skulls and waving his arm for the rest to follow.

The battle turned, and now the settlers were on the offensive; the Comanches fell back consistently until they reached their camp and in confusion began to retreat. The settlers with the white horseman in the lead relentlessly pursued them until they drove the last one from the Cerro del Canadá. By sundown there was not a single live Comanche in Tomé, and the settlers had not lost a single man although there were many wounded. Happy to have saved their families from extermination, they looked around for the man on the white horse in order to thank him, but he was nowhere to be found. They first thought he might have been a Spanish soldier from a nearby garrison, but at last they realized that the Spanish patron saint of battle had come to even the odds when they called upon him at the start of the fight: "Santiago!"

An older tradition relates to Fray Juan de Padilla, who died probably in 1542; he was murdered as soon as the expedition of Francisco Vásquez de Coronado was conveniently out of sight on its return to Mexico. The missionary had elected to stay behind and preach to the Indians, but the Indians had other plans. The priests and medicine men resented anyone who would undermine their prestige by introducing another god more powerful than the one they appealed to with their weird incantations. So long as the protective sword of the Spanish conqueror was raised alongside of the cross, the Indians remained acquiescent and even receptive, but when the swords were sheathed and the expedition marched southward to report to the Viceroy, they lost no time in erasing all evidence of the Europeans' visit. As Fray Juan de Padilla was a serious threat to the shamans, and a living

symbol of the men they hated, he was set upon with clubs and destroyed.

The persistent old padre seems to have won out eventually despite the objections of the priests. Legend says that Indians from the friendly pueblo of Isleta carried his body to their village, placed it in a cottonwood tree log, and buried it under the altar of their church. But Fray de Padilla was not content to stay there; the restlessness that brought him to the Southwest hovers around him after four centuries, and every twelve, or seven, or twenty-seven years, according to the vagaries of tradition, he rises through the floor of the church and must be buried anew.

The people of Isleta say that at certain times of the year his ghost walks around the village, and that anyone who sees him during one of these nocturnal wanderings will die before the year is out. In the days when the Isleta church had nothing but an earthen floor, the padre announced his emergence by wide cracks on the surface, followed by his casket as it gradually pushed its way up. During his appearance in 1911, some of the village Indians removed bits of his cassock for fetishes. They reported that the padre's face was intact, still wearing a long black beard.

In 1921 Winifred Hawkridge Dixon wrote in *Scribner's Magazine* that she had seen the nails coming up in the wooden floor. She added that the phenomenon was "well authenticated and attested by a cardinal, an archbishop, a governor and other dignitaries, to say nothing of Juan Pablo, a man who doesn't lie. It is probably the oldest ghost in the United States."

Those who have investigated the periodic emergence of the Isleta Priest, as he has come to be known, explain it as a phenomenon resulting from the undercurrent of the Río Grande, which runs back of the village. At one time the site of Isleta was an island, as the name indicates, and there are still undercurrents, which during the high water season exert the pressure that forces the casket through the floor of the church. This is the prosaic explanation given to an otherwise interesting appearance of a man identified in legend with the first European martyr in what is now the United States.

CHAPTER 15

HEIRLOOMS OF TRADITION

◆

AN ENTERPRISING SALESMAN who was having a none too easy time peddling home remedies, cosmetics, and other miscellany during the early twenties, decided to try bartering his products for chickens, eggs, and any other farm products available in the out-of-the-way mountain villages of New Mexico. One day while trying to convince one of his lady customers that the face cream he was offering to trade would remove unsightly blemishes, his eye fell upon a flock of noisy chickens trying to drink from a concave-bottomed pan in the back yard. In order to reach the water in the bottom they would hop on the rim of the pan and rock precariously as they reached down for a beakful of water.

Intrigued by this peculiar watering pan, the salesman asked the farm woman where she had got such a strange receptacle, and she replied that her boys had found it in the nearby arroyo after a storm. It had lain around the yard for some time until she decided to put it to a useful purpose. Overcome with curiosity, the salesman asked the señora if she would object to his looking at it more closely. It was a thick piece of metal with a curved bottom and a ridge down the center with several slits along the edges of both ends. After a close examination he offered to trade some of his wares for it, but the lady would not take anything except a new watering pan. The salesman agreed, and a few days later returned with a modern vessel to replace the strange-looking object in the backyard.

The salesman was not altogether surprised, after cleaning and polishing his new acquisition, to find that it was a breastplate of seventeenth century Spanish armor. The chickens could now drink without doing acrobatics, the farm woman was happy with a new watering pan, and the salesman had added one more interesting piece to his growing collection of colonial objects picked up during his business travels.

Many valuable pieces, which have gone into art collections in the Southwest, have been discovered in much the same fashion as this breastplate. Notable among these are the silver mugs, spoons, and platters in the fine collection at the University of New Mexico. Imaginative writers now and then embroider romantic-sounding tales about heirlooms of noble families handed down through countless generations, but in reality most of the silver pieces have been found among the peasant population, whose practical sense has put such articles to useful purposes, even if it is an old piece of Spanish armor for a watering pan in the chicken yard.

One of the largest articles in the Field Collection of old Spanish-Mexican art at the University of New Mexico is a wash basin of solid silver. When it was found in a simple home, it was a tarnished basin where many a face had been refreshed for no one knew how long. Now brightly polished it makes a beautiful exhibition piece displayed in a glass case in an art collection.

Many mountain dwellings in the upper Río Grande have been denuded of colonial *trasteros, vargueños,* and *santos* since the advent of art collectors after World War I. Occasionally one may run across an interesting piece in a remote place where the word may not have reached about the value of antiques, but by and large almost everyone has become conscious of the salability of such objects.

Not many treasures in the way of books have been found in New Mexico because of the relatively small number of literate inhabitants in colonial days, but once in a while a few volumes brought over from Europe found their way eventually into the bottom of some old chest, or were handed down in families with a long survival record. In 1929 I was collecting traditional lore in northern New Mexico, and in the course of my travels was told about a man who used to stage plays in one of the mountain villages near Las Vegas. My traveling companion, Don Rafael Lucero, knew the *ranchito* where this man lived, and one day he took me up there to meet his friend, the producer. We found the old gentleman hoeing his cornfield. After the usual introduction he invited us over to his house near the village of El Chaperito. He presented us to his señora, and when we had accepted the chairs offered us, he asked her:

"Say, Petra, what ever became of that book of *comedias* we used to have around the house?"

Doña Petra thought for a moment and shook her head slowly. Her husband refreshed her memory.

"You remember. The one by Don Pedro."

"Oh yes, I know which one you mean," she answered. "I think it's in that old *baúl* under the bedstead."

She walked over to the adjoining bedroom, pulled out a low chest from under the *cama alta,* and opened it. I should have preferred to look over her shoulder at the contents of the chest, but I kept at a discreet distance as the lady took out little bundles wrapped in cloth and looked them over carefully one by one. Finally she found the book, carefully replaced the articles she had taken out, and closed the chest and pushed it back under the bed. When the book was placed before us on the table, our host put a pair of silver-rimmed glasses on the end of his sunburned nose and began scanning the pages, his lips moving as he held it far back from his face. Satisfied that it was what he wanted, he handed to me saying:

"Please pardon the condition it's in. The mice and the *polillas* have eaten most of the covers, but you can still read it. It's difficult to read because the writer makes a lot of mistakes in spelling. I got used to it eventually and managed to figure it out. It contains very good moral lessons."

I took the book and began leafing through it. On the inside cover I read part of the title, which the mice and worms had spared. The words "Don Pedro . . ." on the first line were followed by part of a title which I recognized as *Autos Sacramentales,* short religious plays by Don Pedro Calderón de la Barca, Spain's leading dramatist of the seventeenth century. I did not have the opportunity to ascertain what edition it was, but from the manner in which the mountaineer had come by it I was almost certain that it was a very early one, possibly a first edition. It had been in the family for a long time. His grandfather had inherited it from *his* grandfather, who according to the present owner was greatly interested in literature. Other books such as the one by "Don Pedro" may still be resting in the bottom of some old chest under a bed in a New Mexican mountaineer's home, where some day by chance someone may discover them.

In the spring of 1930 I had better luck in securing a manuscript, which although not as old as the religious mystery plays of Don Pedro, was quite valuable because it dealt with the death of Kit Carson, the frontiersman. A stamp collector from Detroit, came to Albuquerque about 1929 and began visiting ghost towns and abandoned buildings hoping to find old letters left behind by occupants now long dead. He came to live with one of my neighbors to whom he was related, and after we became acquainted he asked to go along on some of my travels throughout the state. Through some of the members of that large and hoary fraternity of philatelists, he had heard that there was an abandoned post office in the village of Ojo Caliente across from Taos Junction.

My friend volunteered to take his own car when he learned that I was planning to drive to Taos. As Ojo Caliente was not far off my route, we drove up to the former bath resort town and had little difficulty in locating an abandoned wooden shack that in territorial days had served as a post office. The walls were papered with old newspapers, and in the accumulation of trash and debris we found a carton with a few old letters. My friend, who knew stamps better than I did, picked up a number of envelopes that he considered valuable.

"Oh, here's a two-cent stamp that is really good! And take a look at this commemorative issue! What a find!"

The only cachet that aroused my curiosity was one marked "Pony Express." My friend kept that one too. But I came across a neatly folded manuscript written in Spanish and bearing the title: *"A la Muerte del Finado Kit Carson,"* (On the Death of the Late Kit Carson.) It was an elegy written by someone who simply signed his name: "Un amigo." It wasn't bad verse, somewhat reminiscent of the Spanish romantic school of lyric poetry, very ornate, elegant, and replete with emotional figures of speech. The opening lines read in translation:

> Oh thou symbol of true friendship
> Whose new home is now in Heaven. . . .

At the bottom of the last page was the date:

San Fernando de Taos, New Mexico. Mayo 22 de 1869.

BIBLIOGRAPHY

BOOKS

Arnold, Oren. *Ghost Gold*. San Antonio, Texas, The Naylor Company, 1954.

Bancroft, Hubert Howe. *History of Arizona and New Mexico*. Vol. XVII in *The Works of Hubert Howe Bancroft*. San Francisco, A. L. Bancroft and Company, 1889–1890.

Bartlett, John Russell. *Personal Narratives and Incidents in Texas, New Mexico, California, Sonora, and Chihuahua*. 2 vols. New York, D. Appleton, 1856.

Bolton, Herbert Eugene, ed. *Spanish Exploration in the Southwest, 1542–1706*. New York, Charles Scribner's Sons, 1916.

Brevoort, Elias. *New Mexico: Her Natural Resources and Attractions*. Santa Fe, Published by the author, 1874.

Campa, Arthur L. *Los Comanches: A New Mexican Folk Drama*. University of New Mexico *Bulletin*, Modern Language Series, Vol. VII, No. 1 (April, 1942).

——. *Spanish Folk Poetry in New Mexico*. Albuquerque, University of New Mexico Press, 1940.

Ellis, Amanda M. *Legends and Tales of the Rockies*. Colorado Springs, Colorado, Denton Printing Company, 1954.

Griggs, George. *History of the Mesilla Valley and the Gadsden Purchase*. Mesilla, New Mexico, privately published, 1930.

——. *Mines of Chihuahua*. Chihuahua, Mexico, privately published, 1911.

Hackett, Charles Wilson, ed. and trans. *Historical Documents Relating to New Mexico, Nueva Vizcaya, and Approaches Thereto, to 1773.* 3 vols. Washington, Carnegie Institution, 1923–1937.

Hallenbeck, Cleve. *Land of the Conquistadores.* Caldwell, Idaho, Caxton Printers Ltd., 1950.

Inman, Henry. *Stories of the Old Santa Fé Trail.* Kansas City, Missouri, Millet and Hudson, 1881.

———. *The Old Santa Fé Trail.* New York, N. Y., Macmillan, 1897.

James, Henry. *The Curse of San Andres.* New York, Pageant Press, 1953.

Lockwood, Frank C. *Pioneer Days in Arizona.* New York, Macmillan, 1952.

Miller, Joseph. *New Mexico: A Guide to the Colorful State.* New York, Hastings House, 1953.

Montes de Oca, José. *San Agustín Acólmán.* Mexico, D. F. Talleres Gráficos de la Nación, 1929.

Moorhead, Max L. *New Mexico's Royal Road: Trade and Travel on the Chihuahua Trail.* Norman, University of Oklahoma Press, 1958.

Mowry, Sylvester. *The Geography and Resources of Arizona and Sonora.* New York, American Geographical and Statistical Society, 1859 (Washington, Henry Polkinhorn, 1859).

Northrop, Stuart A. *Minerals of New Mexico.* Albuquerque, University of New Mexico Press, 1944.

Ocaranza, Fernando. *Crónica y Relaciónes del Occidente de México.* Vol. II. Mexico, Biblioteca Historica de México de Obras Inéditas, Porrua, 1930.

———. *Establecimientos Franciscanos en el Misterioso Reino de Nueva México.* Mexico, D. F., Mexico, published by the author, 1954.

Pérez de Ribas, Andrés. *Triunfos de Nuestra Santa Fe.* Vol. I. Mexico, D. F., Mexico, Editorial "Layac," 1944.

Raymond, Rossiter Worthington. *Statistics of Mines and Mining in the Territories West of the Rocky Mountains.* Washington, Government Printing Office, 1870.

Rickard, Thomas A. *A History of American Mining.* New York, Mc-Graw-Hill, 1932.

Ruxton, George F. *Adventures in Mexico and the Rocky Mountains.* New York, Harper Brothers, 1855.

Twichell, Ralph Emerson. *The Leading Facts of New Mexican History.* 5 vols. Cedar Rapids, Iowa, The Torch Press, 1911–1917.

Wolle, Muriel Sibell. *The Bonanza Trail: Ghost Towns and Mining Camps of the West.* Bloomington, Indiana University Press, 1953.

ARTICLES

Crawford, R. W. "Mysterious Gold Mine of El Paso County," *Hunter's Frontier Magazine,* Vol. I, No. 6 (October, 1916).

Goetz, Otto. "Caballo Treasure," *New Mexico,* Vol. XVIII, No. 1 (March, 1940), 14–15.

Goodspeed, Edgar J. "Old Chest Found in the Mountains," *El Palacio Magazine,* Vol. XII, No. 6 (June, 1922), 142–43.

Hawkridge, Winifred Dixon. "The Oldest Ghost in the United States," *Scribner's Magazine,* Vol. 71, No. 2 (August, 1921), 125.

Le Noir, Phil. "The Hermit of Las Vegas," *Publications of the Texas Folklore Society,* X (1932), 124–26.

Livingston, Carl. "Secrets of the Guadalupes," *New Mexico Highway Journal,* Vol. IX, No. 1 (January, 1929), 9–11.

Lummis, Charles F. "The Cities That Were Forgotten," *Scribner's Magazine,* Vol. 13, No. 4 (April, 1893), 466.

Schoonmaker, Rodney B. "Missionary Gave Name to Hermit's Peak," *Las Vegas Daily Optic,* June 3, 1939.

Strickfaden, William H. "Hermit's Peak and the Crosses," *New Mexico Sun Trails,* Vol. X, No. 3 (August, 1952), 15.

MANUSCRIPTS

Brown, Lorin W. "Treasures of New Mexico." Manuscript in WPA files, State Museum, Santa Fe, New Mexico.

Gerdeman, W. A. "Chapter in the History of Las Vegas." Unpublished manuscript prepared in 1948 for American History Seminar at Highlands University, Las Vegas, New Mexico.

Salgado, Juan Lorenzo. "Letters Written to the Jesuit Provincial Ygnacio Calderon." National Archives, Mexico, D. F., Mexico.

Wolfe, Charles. "The History of the 'Wonder of our Century.'" St. Michael's College, Santa Fe, New Mexico.

INDEX

Treasure of the Sangre de Cristos has been set in various sizes of Linotype Granjon, designed in 1924 by George W. Jones. In the years since its creation, Granjon has become one of the most popular faces used in books, which is a tribute to the honest design and legibility distinguishing this type.

UNIVERSITY OF OKLAHOMA PRESS

NORMAN

CPSIA information can be obtained at www.ICGtesting.com
Printed in the USA
LVOW120149130313

323926LV00001B/3/A